This **was the kind of desire he'd missed for so long.**

Urgent and hot. Utterly compelling. As if he couldn't envisage getting off this plane and *not* taking Sidonie with him so that he could taste her all over.

'Er…excuse me, Mr Christakos?'

He looked up and there she was. Just like that any semblance of clear-headedness was gone and he was reduced to animal lust again. He had to get up and let her back in, cursing his body which would not obey his head.

One thing he was sure of as she brushed past him in the small space and her scent tantalised him: he wanted this Sidonie Fitzgerald with a hunger he'd not known before. And he would have her. Because Alexio Christakos always got what he wanted.

BLOOD BROTHERS
Power and passion run in their veins

Rafaele and Alexio have learned that to feel emotion is to be weak. Calculated ruthlessness brings them immense success in the boardroom and in the bedroom. But a storm is coming with the sudden appearance of a long-lost half-brother, Cesar, and three women who will change their lives for ever…

*Read **Rafaele Falcone's** story in:*
WHEN FALCONE'S WORLD STOPS TURNING
February 2014

Only one woman has come close to touching this brooding Italian's cold heart, and he intends to have her once more. But Samantha Rourke has a secret that will rock his world in a very different way…

*Read **Alexio Christakos's** story in:*
WHEN CHRISTAKOS MEETS HIS MATCH
April 2014

His legendary Greek charm can get him any woman he wants—and he wants Sidonie Fitzgerald for one, hot night. But when that night isn't enough will he regret breaking his own rules?

*And read **Cesar Da Silva's** story in:*
WHEN DA SILVA BREAKS THE RULES
June 2014

The prodigal son is tormented by his dark past. Can one woman save this Spanish billionaire's tortured soul, or is he beyond redemption?

WHEN CHRISTAKOS MEETS HIS MATCH

BY
ABBY GREEN

Published in Great Britain 2014
by Mills & Boon, an imprint of Harlequin (UK) Limited,
Eton House, 18-24 Paradise Road, Richmond, Surrey, TW9 1SR

ISBN: 978 0 263 24198 3

Harlequin (UK) Limited's policy is to use papers that are natural,
renewable and recyclable products and made from wood grown in
sustainable forests. The logging and manufacturing processes conform
to the legal environmental regulations of the country of origin.

Printed and bound in Great Britain
by CPI Antony Rowe, Chippenham, Wiltshire

Abby Green spent her teens reading Mills and Boon® romances. After repeatedly deferring a degree to study Social Anthropology (long story...) she ended up working for many years in the film and TV Industry as an assistant director.

One day, while standing outside an actor's trailer, waiting for him to emerge, in the rain, holding an umbrella in gale force winds, she thought to herself, *Surely there's more than this—and it involves being inside and dry?*

Thinking of her love for Mills and Boon, and encouraged by a friend, Abby decided to submit a partial manuscript. After numerous rewrites, chucking out the original idea and starting again with a new story, her first book was accepted and an author was born.

She is happy to report that days of standing in the rain outside an actor's trailer are a rare occurrence now. She loves creating stories that will put you through an emotional wringer (in a good way, hopefully), yet leave you feeling satisfied and uplifted.

She lives in Dublin, Ireland, and you can find out more about her and her books here: www.abby-green.com

Recent titles by the same author:

WHEN FALCONE'S WORLD STOPS TURNING
  (Blood Brothers)
FORGIVEN BUT NOT FORGOTTEN?
EXQUISITE REVENGE
ONE NIGHT WITH THE ENEMY

Did you know these are also available as eBooks?
Visit www.millsandboon.co.uk

*I'd like to dedicate this book to all the
fabulous Harlequin Mills and Boon
readers and fans who make my job so much easier,
especially on the days when the task can seem impossible!*

PROLOGUE

ALEXIO CHRISTAKOS HAD always known his mother had had affairs all through her marriage to his father. He just hadn't expected to see such a public display of it at her funeral. Her coffin was strewn with lone flowers and there were displays of wet eyes from a handful of men he'd never met before in his life.

His father had stomped away with a glower on his face a short while before. He couldn't exactly claim the moral high ground as he too had had numerous affairs.

It had been a constant war of attrition between them. His father always seeking to make his mother as jealous as he felt. And she…? Alexio had the feeling that nothing would have ever made her truly happy, even though she had lived her life in the lap of luxury, surrounded by people to cater to her every whim.

She'd had a sadness, a deep melancholy about her, and they'd never been emotionally close. A vivid memory assailed him at that moment—a memory he hadn't allowed to surface for a long time. He'd been about nine, and his throat had ached with the effort it had taken not to cry. He'd just witnessed his parents having a bitter row.

His mother had caught him standing behind the door and he'd blurted out, 'Why do you hate each other so much? Why can't you be in love like you're supposed to be?'

She'd looked at him coldly and the lack of emotion in

her eyes had made him shiver. She'd bent down to his level and taken his chin in her hand. 'Love's a fairytale, Alexio, and it doesn't exist. Remember this: I married your father because he could give me what I needed. *That's* what is important. Success. Security. Power. Don't ever concern yourself with emotions. They make you weak. Especially love.'

Alexio would never forget the excoriating feeling of exposure and shame in that moment…

He felt a hand on his shoulder then and looked to his older half-brother, Rafaele, who stood beside him and smiled tightly. They'd always shared the same conflicted relationship with their mother. Rafaele's Italian father had gone to pieces after their mother had walked out on him when he had lost his entire fortune—an unpalatable reminder of their mother's ruthless nature so soon after that disturbing childhood memory of his own.

For years Alexio and his brother had communicated with habitual boyish rough-housing and rivalry, but since Rafaele had left home to make his way when Alexio had been about fourteen their relationship had become less fractious. Even if Alexio had never quite been able to let go of his envy that Rafaele hadn't had to endure the almost suffocating attention he'd received from his father. The heavy weight of expectation. The disappointment when Alexio had been determined to prove himself and not accept his inheritance.

They turned to walk away from the grave, engrossed in their own thoughts. They were of a similar build and height, both a few inches over six feet, drop-dead gorgeous, dark-haired. Alexio's hair was darker, cut close to his skull. Their mother had bequeathed to them both her distinctive green eyes, but Alexio's were lighter—more golden.

When they came to a stop near the cars Alexio decided to rib his brother gently, seeking to assuage the suddenly bleak feeling inside him. He observed his brother's stubbled jaw. 'You couldn't even clean up for the funeral?'

'I got out of bed too late,' Rafaele drawled with a glint in his eye.

Alexio smiled wryly. 'Unbelievable. You've only been in Athens for two days—no wonder you wanted to stay at a hotel and not at my apartment...'

Rafaele was about to respond when Alexio saw his face close up and his eyes narrow on something or someone behind him. He turned to look too and saw a tall, stern-faced stranger staring at them from a few feet away. Something struck him in the gut: recognition. Crazy. But the man's eyes were a distinctive green...and that gut feeling intensified.

The stranger flicked a glance at the grave behind them and then his lip curled. 'Are there any more of us?'

Alexio bristled at his belligerent tone and frowned, '*Us*? What are you talking about?'

The man just looked at Rafaele. 'You don't remember, do you?'

Alexio saw Rafaele go pale. Hoarsely he asked, 'Who are you?'

The man smiled, but it was cold, 'I'm your older brother—*half-brother*. My name is Cesar da Silva. I came today to pay my respects to the woman who gave me life... not that she deserved it.'

He was still talking but a roaring was sounding in Alexio's ears. *Older half-brother? Cesar da Silva.* He'd heard of the man. Who hadn't? He was the owner of a vast global conglomerate encompassing real estate, finance—myriad businesses. Famously private and reclusive.

Something rose up inside Alexio and he issued an abrupt, 'What the *hell*?'

The man looked at him coldly and Alexio could now see the fraternal similarities that had led to that prickle of awareness. Even though da Silva was dark blond in colouring, they could be non-identical triplets.

Da Silva was saying coldly, 'Three brothers by three fathers…and yet she didn't abandon either of *you* to the wolves.'

He stepped forward and Alexio immediately stepped up too, feeling rage building inside him in the face of this shocking revelation. His half-brother topped him only by an inch at most. They stood chest to chest.

Cesar gritted out, 'I didn't come here to fight you, brother. I have no issue with either of you.'

A fierce well of protectiveness that Alexio had felt once before for his mother, before she'd rejected it, rose up within him. 'Only with our dead mother—*if* what you say is true.'

Cesar smiled, but it was bleak, and it threw Alexio off slightly, making the rage diminish.

'Oh, it's true—more's the pity.'

He stepped around him then and Alexio and Rafaele turned to watch him walk to the open grave, where he stood for a few long moments before taking something from his pocket and throwing it into the black space, where it landed with a dull thud.

Eventually he turned and came back. After a long, silent but charged moment, during which he looked at both brothers, he turned and walked swiftly to a waiting car. He got into the back. It drove off smoothly.

Rafaele turned towards Alexio and looked at him. Gobsmacked. Shock reverberated through his body. Adrenalin made him feel keyed up.

'What the…?'

Rafaele just shook his head. 'I don't know…'

Alexio looked back at the empty space where the car had been and something cold settled into his belly. He felt exposed, remembering that time when he'd thought his mother would allow him to protect her. She hadn't. Ever elusive, she was now managing to reach out from beyond the grave and demonstrate with dramatic timing just how a woman couldn't be trusted to tell the truth and reveal her secrets. She would always hold something back. Something that might have the power to shatter your world.

CHAPTER ONE

Five months later...

'*Cara*...DO YOU have to leave so soon?'

The voice oozed sultry sex appeal. Alexio stalled for a second in the act of buttoning up his shirt—not because he was tempted to stay but because, if anything, he felt even more eager to leave.

He schooled his features and turned to face the woman in the bed. She was all honeyed limbs and artfully tumbled glossy brown hair. Huge dark eyes, a pouting mouth and the absence of a sheet were doing little to help Alexio forget why he'd chosen to take her to his hotel suite in Milan after his brother Rafaele's wedding reception last night.

She was stunning. Perfect.

Even so, he felt no resurgence of desire. And Alexio didn't like to acknowledge the fact that the sex had been wholly underwhelming. On the surface it had been fine; but on some deeper level it had left him cold. He switched on the charm he was famed for, though, and smiled.

'Sorry, *bellissima*, I have to fly to Paris this morning for work.'

The woman, whose name he all of a sudden wasn't entirely sure of—Carmela?—leant back and stretched seductively, displaying her perfectly cosmetically enhanced naked breasts to their best advantage, and pouted even more. 'You have to leave *right now*?'

Alexio kept his smile in place and when he'd finished dressing bent down and pressed a light kiss to her mouth, escaping before she could twine her arms around his neck. Claustrophobia was rising within him.

'We had fun, *cara*…I'll call you.'

Now the seductive pout was gone, and the woman's real nature shone through as her eyes turned hard. She knew when she was being blown off and clearly did not like it when the man in question was as sought-after as Alexio Christakos.

She stood up from the bed naked and flounced off to the bathroom, issuing a stream of Italian petulance. Alexio winced slightly but let out a sigh of relief as soon as she'd disappeared behind a slamming door.

He shook his head as he made his way out of the suite and towards the lobby of the plush hotel in the private lift reserved for VIP guests. *Women*. He loved them, but he loved them at a distance. In his bed when it suited him and then out of it for as long as he cared to indulge them—which invariably wasn't for long.

After years of witnessing his mother's cold behaviour towards his father, who had remained in slavish thrall to her beauty and eternal elusiveness, Alexio had developed a very keen sense of self-protection around women. He could handle cold and aloof because he was used to that, and he preferred it.

His father, thwarted by his emotionally unavailable wife, had turned to his son, making him the centre of his world. It had been too much. From an early age Alexio had chafed against the claustrophobia of his father's over-attention. And now when anyone—especially a woman—became even remotely over-emotional, or expected too much, he shut down inside.

Brief encounters were his forté. Witnessing his half-brother's wedding the day before had inevitably brought up questions of his own destiny, but Alexio, at the age of thirty, felt no compelling need to settle down yet.

He did envisage a wife and family at some stage…far in the future. When the time came his wife would be perfect. Beautiful, accommodating. Undemanding of Alexio's emotions. Above all, Alexio would not fall into the same trap as his father: tortured for life because he'd coveted a woman who didn't covet him. He'd been disabused at an early age of the notion that love might be involved.

He thought of his older brother turning up at his mother's funeral and all the accompanying unwelcome emotions he'd felt that day: shock, anger, hurt, betrayal.

Used to blocking out emotions, Alexio had relegated the incident to the back of his mind. He hadn't sought Cesar da Silva out, hadn't mentioned it again to Rafaele—even though he knew Rafaele had invited their half-brother to his wedding. Predictably enough, after that first and last terse meeting, he hadn't turned up.

Emotions were messy, unpredictable. They tripped you up. Look at Rafaele! His life had just been turned upside down by a woman who had kept his son from him for four years. And yet two months after meeting her again he was getting married, looking foolishly in love and blithely forgetting the lessons his own father had taught him about the fickle nature of women.

As far as Alexio was concerned—even if Rafaele appeared to be happily embarking on wedded bliss, and no matter how cute his three-and-a-half-year-old nephew was—his brother had been played for a fool by his new wife. Why *wouldn't* she now want to marry Rafaele Falcone, *wunderkind* of the worldwide automobile industry, with an estimated wealth running into the billions? Especially if she had a son to support?

No, Alexio was steering well clear of similar scenarios and he would never allow himself to be caught as his brother had been. He would never forgive a woman who kept a child from him. Still, a sliver of unease went down his spine. His brother, whom he'd considered to share a similar philosophy, had managed to get caught…

Alexio's mouth firmed and he pushed such rogue notions down deep. He put on a pair of shades as his driver brought the car around to the front entrance and was oblivious to the double-take stares of a group of women as they walked into the hotel.

As soon as the car pulled away Alexio was already focusing on the next thing on his agenda, the introspection his brother's wedding had precipitated along with his recent unsatisfactory bed partner already relegated to the back of his mind.

Sidonie Fitzgerald buckled her seatbelt on the plane and took a deep breath. But she was unable to shift the ball of tension sitting in her belly. For once her habitual fear of flying was being eclipsed by something else, and Sidonie couldn't even really enjoy that fact.

All she could see in her mind's eye was her beloved Tante Josephine's round, eternally childish and worried face and hear her quavering voice: *'Sidonie, what does it mean? Will they take my home from me? All these bills… where did they come from?'*

Sidonie's aunt was fifty-four and had spent a lifetime locked in a world of innocence. She'd been deprived of oxygen as a baby and as a result had been mildly brain-damaged. She'd always functioned at a slightly lesser and slower level than everyone around her, but had managed to get through school and find a job. She still worked in the grocer's shop around the corner from where she'd lived for years, giving her precious independence.

Sidonie pursed her lips. She had loved her self-absorbed and endlessly vain mother, who had passed away only a couple of months before, but how could her mother have done this to her sweet and innocent younger sister?

The never forgotten sting of shame reminded Sidonie all too uncomfortably of *exactly* how her mother could have done such a thing—as if she could ever really forget. Ruthlessly she quashed it.

When Sidonie's father had died a few years before, their comfortable lives had crashed around their ears, leaving them with nothing. Sidonie had been forced to leave her university degree before the start of her final year in order to find work and save money to go back.

Moving to Paris to live with Tante Josephine had been her mother Cecile's only option to avoid becoming homeless or—even worse—having to find *work*. Cecile had not been happy. She'd been used to a life of comfort, relative luxury and security, courtesy of her hard-working husband who had wanted nothing more than to make his wife happy.

It would appear now, though, as if Sidonie's mother's selfish ways had risen to the fore again. She'd encouraged her sister to take out a mortgage on the apartment that had been bought and paid for by her husband because he'd cared for his vulnerable sister-in-law's welfare. Cecile had used this fact as leverage to persuade Tante Josephine to agree to the remortgage. She'd then used that money, and credit cards in both their names, to spend a small fortune. Tante Josephine now found herself liable for the astronomical bills as the remaining living account-holder.

Sidonie had to figure out the best way forward to help her aunt—she had no intention of leaving her to fend for herself. The start of the process had been taking on the burden of the debts into her own name. She hadn't thought twice about doing it—ever since her childhood innocence had been ripped away Sidonie had developed a well-ingrained instinct to cover up for her mother—even now, when she was gone.

Sidonie was facing the prospect of moving to Paris to help her aunt get out of this crisis. She staved off the sense of panic. She was young and healthy. Surely she could get work? Even if it was menial?

In a sick way events had conspired to help her—she'd lost her waitressing job in Dublin just before she'd left for Paris to meet with a solicitor to discuss her aunt's situation. Her restaurant boss had explained miserably that they had gone into liquidation, like so many others. Sidonie was going back to Dublin now—just to tie up loose ends and collect the deposit owed to her on her flat when she moved out.

Her hands clenched into fists at the thought of how her mother had only ever thought about herself, oblivious to the repercussions of her—

'Here is your seat, sir.'

'Thank you.'

Sidonie's thoughts scattered as she heard the exchange above her head, and she looked up and saw a man. She blinked. And blinked again. He was very tall and broad. Slim hips at her eye level. He was taking off an overcoat and folding it up to place it in the overheard locker, revealing a lean, muscular build under a fine silk shirt and jacket. Sidonie was vaguely aware of the way the air hostess was hovering attentively.

The man said in English, with a seductive foreign accent, 'I've got it, thank you.'

The air hostess looked comically deflated and turned away. The man was now taking off his suit jacket, and Sidonie realised she was staring—no better than the gaping air hostess. Quickly she averted her head and looked out of the window, seeing nothing of the pewter-grey Parisian spring skies and the fluorescent-jacket-clad ground staff preparing the plane for take-off.

His image was burned onto her brain. It didn't help when she felt him take the seat beside her and all the air around them seemed to disappear. And it *really* didn't help when his scent teased her nostrils; musky and masculine.

He was quite simply the most gorgeous man she'd ever seen in her life. Dark olive complexion, high cheekbones, strong jaw. Short dark brown hair. Firmly sculpted masculine mouth. He should have been pretty. But Sidonie's impression was not of *pretty*. It was of hard and uncompromising sexuality. *Heat.* The last kind of person she'd have expected to sit in an economy seat beside her.

And then he spoke. 'Excuse me.'

His voice was so deep that she felt it reverberate in the pit of her belly. She swallowed and told herself she was being ridiculous—he couldn't possibly be *that* gorgeous. She turned her head and her heart stopped. His face was inches away. He *was*…that gorgeous. And more. He looked vaguely familiar and she wondered if he was a famous male model. Or a French movie star?

Something funny was happening to Sidonie's brain and body. They didn't seem to be connected any more. She felt a hysterical giggle rise up and had to stifle it. She didn't giggle. What was wrong with her?

One dark brow moved upwards over the most startling pair of green eyes she'd ever seen. Gold and green. Like a lion. She had green eyes too, but they were more blue than green.

'I think you're sitting on my seatbelt?'

It took a few seconds for the words to compute, and when they did Sidonie jumped up as if scalded, hands flapping. 'I'm so sorry… Excuse me… Just let me… It must be here somewhere…'

Sounding irritated, the man said, 'Stay still and I'll get it.'

Sidonie closed her eyes in mortification, her hands gripping the seat-back in front of her, and she hovered, contorted in the small space, as the man coolly retrieved his seatbelt and buckled it.

Sidonie sat down again and attended to her own belt. Feeling breathless, and avoiding looking at him again, she said, 'I'm sorry. I—'

He cut her off. 'It's fine, don't worry about it.'

A flare of something hot lanced Sidonie's belly. Did he *have* to sound so curt? And why was she suddenly so aware of the fact that her hair was scraped up into a messy bun, that she had no make-up on, that she was wearing jeans that were so worn there was a frayed hole at her knee and an equally worn university sweatshirt. And her glasses. If Central Casting had been looking for 'messy grunge student type' she would have been hired on the spot.

She was disgusted at herself for letting a man—albeit a man as gorgeous as this one—make her feel so self-conscious. She forced herself to take a deep breath and looked resolutely forward. Out of the corner of her eye, though, she was aware of big, strong-looking hands opening up a tablet computer. Her belly clenched.

The seconds stretched to minutes and she heard him sigh volubly when the plane still wasn't moving. His arm nearest to her reached up to push something, and she realised it must have been the call button when the stewardess arrived with indecent haste.

'Yes, sir?'

Sidonie heard the irritation in his voice. 'Is there a reason why we're not moving yet?'

She looked over and saw only his strong profile and jaw, and even though she couldn't see it she could imagine the kind of expression he'd be using: imperious. She glanced at the woman and felt sorry for her because she looked so embarrassed.

'I'm not sure, sir. I'll check right away.' She rushed off again.

Sidonie let out a faint snort of derision. Even the stewardess was treating him as if he was some sort of overlord.

He looked at her then. 'I'm sorry… Did you say something?'

Sidonie tried not to be affected by his overwhelming presence. She shrugged minutely. 'I'm sure we're just waiting in line to take our slot on the runway.'

He turned to face her more fully and Sidonie cursed herself. The last thing she needed was his undivided attention on her.

'Oh, really? And what if I have an important meeting to attend in London?'

Something hot flashed into Sidonie's veins and she told herself it was anger at his insufferable arrogance. She crossed her arms in an unconsciously defensive move and said in a low voice, 'Well, in case it's escaped your attention, there are approximately two hundred people on this plane. I'm sure more than one other person has a meeting to make, and I don't see them complaining.'

His eyes flashed and momentarily stopped her breath. They were so unusual and stark against his dark skin. He was like a specimen from some exotic planet.

'There's two hundred and ten, actually, and I don't doubt that there are many others who have important appointments lined up—which makes my question even more relevant.'

Sidonie barely registered the fact that he knew exactly how many were on board and bristled at the way his eyes had done that quick sweep up and down her body, clearly deducing that she *wasn't* on her way to an important meeting.

'For your information,' she said frigidly, 'I have a connecting flight to Dublin from London and I'll be very inconvenienced if we're late. But that's just life, isn't it?'

He leant back a little and looked at her. 'I wondered where your accent was from. It's intriguing.'

Sidonie wasn't sure if that was a compliment or not, so she clamped her mouth shut. Just then someone dressed in uniform with a cap came alongside their seats and coughed slightly to get the man's attention.

Releasing Sidonie from his compelling gaze, the man turned, and the pilot bent down and said discreetly, 'Mr Christakos, sorry about this delay. It's beyond our control, I'm afraid… They've got a backlog of planes waiting to take off. It shouldn't be much longer, but we can get your private jet ready if you'd prefer?'

Sidonie knew her eyes had gone wide as she took in this exchange.

After a few moments the man said, 'No, I'll stay, Pierre. But thank you for thinking of it.'

The captain inclined his head deferentially and left again and Sidonie realised that her mouth was open. Abruptly she shut it and looked out of the window before the man could see. In her line of vision was a similar plane to theirs, standing nearby, with the distinctive Christakos logo emblazoned on the side, along with a quote from a Greek philosopher. All of Alexio Christakos's planes sported quotes.

Alexio Christakos.

Sidonie shook her head minutely, in disbelief. The man next to her—now on his phone, with that deep voice speaking in a language that sounded like Greek—could *not* be the owner of Christakos Freight and Travel. That man was a legend. And he would certainly not be sitting beside her, with his long legs constricted by the confines of economy class seating.

He'd been a case study in their business class at college before she'd had to leave. Astonishingly successful while still disgustingly young, he'd made headlines when he'd cut himself off from his father's inheritance to go his own way, never revealing to anyone his reasons for doing so.

He'd then grafted and worked his way up, starting up an online freight company that had blown all of the competition out of the water, and when he'd sold it after only two years he'd made a fortune. It was that early success that had given him the finances to branch out into air travel, and within the space of five years he'd been competing with and beating the best budget airlines in Europe. He had a reputation for treating customers like people and not like herded cattle, which was a trademark of a lot of Christakos's competition.

He was also one of the most eligible bachelors in Europe, if not the world. Sidonie was not a gossip magazine aficionado, but after they'd studied his entrepreneurial methods in college she'd had to listen to her fellow classmates wax lyrical about the man, drooling over copious pictures of him, for weeks. With a sinking feeling in her chest, she realised why he looked vaguely familiar. Even though she'd not shared in their collective drooling she'd glanced at a couple of pictures, dismissing him as a pretty boy.

Now she knew: pretty he was *not*. He was all male. Virile and potent. She felt like squirming, and she wanted to change seats. She was suddenly acutely uncomfortable and didn't like to analyse why that might be. She wasn't used to someone having such an immediate physical effect on her.

The woman in the seat next to Alexio was starting to fidget. He had to curb the urge to put his hand on her thigh to stop her and curled that hand into a fist. She was clearly a nervy sort from the way she'd reacted when she discovered she was sitting on his seatbelt.

It was intensely irritating to him that he was aware of her at all. That he'd done a minor double-take on hearing her challenge him. He chafed at being in such close confines with another person after years of the luxury of private air travel, but if he wasn't so damned conscientious… *and controlling*… His mouth quirked at the thought of the insult that had been hurled his way more than once.

On the phone, his assistant was informing him of his schedule in London, but Alexio caught sight of a sliver of pale knee peeping out of torn jeans beside him and stifled a snort. Could she be *any* messier? He'd taken in an impression after exchanging those few words—light-coloured hair, a slim body, pale face, glasses. Voluminous sweatshirt that hid any trace of femininity. And a surprisingly husky voice with that intriguing accent.

Alexio did not take notice of women who did not dress like women. He had high standards after being brought up by one of the world's foremost models. His mother had always been impeccably turned out. He frowned. He was thinking of her *again*.

Realising the novel fact that he was not actually taking in a word his assistant was saying, Alexio terminated the conversation abruptly. The woman went still beside him and something tensed inside him. He could be on his way to his private jet right now but he'd refused. Again, not like him. But something had stopped him. Something in his gut.

He glanced over to see that the woman had a capacious grey bag on her lap and was pulling things out of the seat pocket in front of her to put them in haphazardly. Another strike against her. Alexio was a neat freak. She'd pushed her black-framed glasses on her head and his eye was drawn to her hair.

It was actually strawberry blonde. An intriguing colour. It looked to be wavy and unruly if let loose, and he found himself wondering how long it was when it wasn't confined in that high bun, with wisps curling against her neck and face.

Something tightened inside him, down low. Her face, too, was not as unremarkable as he'd first thought. Heart-shaped and pale. He could see a faint smattering of freckles across her small straight nose and it shocked him slightly. It had been so long since he'd been this close to a face without make-up. It felt curiously intimate.

Her hands were small and quick. Deft. Short, practical nails. And just like that Alexio felt a punch of desire bloom in his gut. It was hot and immediate as he imagined how small and pale those hands would look on his body, caressing him, touching him, stroking him. The images were so incendiary that Alexio's breath stopped for a moment.

The girl seemed to have restored her belongings to her bag and now, almost as an afterthought, she took her glasses off her head and put them in too.

She must be aware of his scrutiny—he could see a flood of red stain her cheeks. And that stunned him anew. When was the last time he'd seen a woman blush?

Alexio leant back slightly, noting that her mouth in profile looked full and soft. Kissable.

'Going somewhere?' he asked, slightly perturbed that his voice sounded so rough.

The woman took a breath, making her sweatshirt rise and fall, drawing his eye to the flesh it concealed. He had a sudden hunger to *see* her. And he wondered about her breasts. That desire increased, shocking him slightly with its force. He'd just left a woman in his hotel suite—what was wrong with him?

She looked at him and Alexio's eyes met hers. He sucked in a breath. Without the black-framed glasses they were stunning. Almond-shaped. Aquamarine. Like the sea around the islands in Greece. Sparkling green one second and blue the next. Long dark lashes were a contrast against her pale colouring, and her eyebrows the same strawberry blonde tone as her hair.

She looked resolute, her hands gripping her bag, that soft mouth tight now, eyes avoiding his. 'I'll move seats.'

Alexio frowned. Everything in his body was rejecting the notion with a force he didn't like to acknowledge. 'Why on earth do you want to move?'

This was another novel experience—a woman trying to get away from him!

Alexio settled back further in his seat. The woman opened her mouth again and he saw small, even white teeth. Her two front teeth had a slight gap in the middle. He had the uncanny feeling that he could just sit there and stare at her for hours.

Now she was blushing in earnest.

'Well, you're obviously…you know…' she looked at him now, slightly agonised.

He quirked a brow. 'What am I?'

Her cheeks went an even brighter red and Alexio had to curb the desire to reach out and touch them to see if they felt as hot as they looked.

She huffed now, impatiently. 'Well, you're obviously *you*, and you have things to do, people to talk to. You need space.'

Something cold settled into Alexio's belly and his eyes narrowed. Of course. She'd heard that exchange with the pilot and would have deduced who he was. Still…in his experience once people knew who he was they didn't try to get away—the opposite, in fact.

'I have all the space I need. You don't need to go anywhere. I'll feel insulted if you move.'

Sidonie had to force herself to calm down. What on earth was wrong with her? So what if he was Alexio Christakos, one of the most powerful entrepreneurs of his time? So what if he was more gorgeous than any man she'd ever seen? Since when had she become a walking hormone, anyway? The flight was only an hour. She could handle anything for an hour. Even sitting beside Alexio Christakos.

She forced herself to relax her grip on her bag and said, in as calm a voice as she could muster, 'Fine. I just thought that in light of…who you are…you might appreciate some more space. I mean physically. You're not exactly…' Sidonie stopped and bit her lip, slid her gaze from his uncomfortably.

In an effort to distract him she started to take stuff out of her bag again: a book, papers…

'I'm not exactly what?'

Sidonie could hear the barely suppressed smile in his voice and it made her prickle at being such an object of humour for him.

'You know very well what I mean…' She waved a hand in his general direction. 'You're not exactly designed to fit into economy class, are you?'

She could have sworn she heard a muffled snort but refused to look, thrusting her bag back down under the seat in front. She hated to acknowledge the zinging sensation in her blood, as if she'd been plugged into a mild electric current.

She sat back and crossed her arms, and looked at him to find him regarding her with a small smile playing around his mouth. *Lord.* Almost accusingly she asked, 'Why are you here anyway? Apparently you could be on a private jet rather than waiting here like the rest of us.'

That green gaze was steady, unsettling.

'It's a spot-check. I like to do them from time to time, to make sure things are running smoothly.'

Sidonie breathed out as something clicked in her brain. 'Of course. I read about that.'

He frowned and she clarified reluctantly, feeling hot and self-conscious. 'You were a case study in my business module at college.'

That information didn't appear to be news to him. 'What else did you study at college?'

Embarrassed now, Sidonie admitted, 'Technically I'm still in college... I had to leave before the start of my final year just over a year ago, due to personal events. I'm saving money to try and complete my course... My degree is in Business and French.'

'What happened?'

Sidonie looked at him. On some level she was shocked at his directness, but it was also curiously refreshing. She couldn't seem to remove her gaze from his. The small space they occupied felt strangely intimate, cocoon-like.

'I... Well, my father lost his construction business when the property boom crashed in Ireland. He struggled for a while but it was useless. He only managed to get himself into debt.' Sidonie went cold inside. 'He passed away not long afterwards. Everything was gone—the business, the house... College was paid for up to a point, but then the money ran out. I had to leave and work.'

Sidonie felt uncomfortable under his gaze. It was intense, unsettling.

'And why were you in Paris?'

Sidonie arched a brow. 'What is this? Twenty questions? What were *you* doing in Paris?'

Alexio crossed his arms and Sidonie's belly clenched when she saw how the muscles in his arm bunched under the thin silk of his shirt. She gulped and looked back into that hypnotising gaze.

'I was in Milan yesterday at my brother's wedding, he said. 'Then I flew to Paris this morning to catch this flight, so that I could do my check while en route to London.'

'Are you not concerned about missing your meeting?'

Alexio smiled and the bottom dropped out of Sidonie's belly.

'It's not ideal, but they'll wait for me.'

Of course they would, she thought faintly. Who wouldn't wait for this man?

'So,' he said patiently, 'now will you tell me why *you* were in Paris?'

Sidonie looked at him and unbidden a lump came to her throat for her wayward. selfish mother and her poor Tante Josephine who was so worried. She swallowed it down.

'I was here to meet with a solicitor to deal with my mother's affairs. She passed away in Paris a couple of months ago. She'd been living with my aunt; she's from here originally.' She corrected herself. '*Was* from here, I mean. She moved back after my father died.'

Alexio uncrossed his arms and his expression sobered. 'That's rough—to lose both parents in such a short space of time. I lost my mother too—five months ago.'

Sidonie's chest tightened. A moment of empathy. Union. 'I'm sorry… It's hard, isn't it?'

His mouth twisted. 'I have to admit that we weren't that close—but, yes, it was still a shock.'

That feeling intensified in Sidonie's chest. She revealed huskily, 'I did love my mum, and I know she loved me, but we weren't that close either. She was very… self-absorbed.'

Suddenly the plane lurched into movement and Sidonie's hands went to grab the armrests automatically as she looked out of the window. 'Oh, God, we're moving.'

A dry voice came from her left. 'That's generally what a plane does before it takes off.'

'Very funny,' muttered Sidonie, and their recent conversation was wiped from her mind as she battled with the habitual fear of flying she faced.

'Hey, are you okay? You look terrible.'

'No,' Sidonie got out painfully, knowing she'd probably gone ashen. Her eyes were closed. 'I'm not okay, but I will be if you just leave me alone. Ignore me.'

'You're scared of flying? And you're taking two flights to Dublin? Why didn't you just take a direct flight?' Now he sounded censorious.

'Because,' Sidonie gritted out, 'it worked out cheaper to do it this way, and the direct flights were all full anyway. It was short notice.'

The familiar nausea started to rise and she clamped her mouth shut, feeling cold and clammy. She tried not to think back to the huge breakfast her Tante Josephine had insisted on them both having before they'd left on their respective journeys. It sat heavily in her belly now.

The plane was moving in earnest; this was always the worst part—and the take-off. And the landing. And sometimes in between if there was turbulence.

'Did something happen to make you scared?'

Sidonie wished he would just ignore her, but bit out, 'What? You mean apart from the fact that I'm miles above the earth, surrounded by nothing but a bit of tin and fibreglass or whatever planes are made of?'

'They're actually made mainly of aluminium, although sometimes a composite of metals is used, and in newer technology they're looking at carbon fibre. My brother designs and builds cars, so we're actually looking into new technologies together.'

Sidonie cracked open one eye and cast Alexio a baleful glance. 'Why are you telling me this?'

'Because your fears are irrational. You *do* know that air travel is the safest form of travel in the world?'

Sidonie opened both eyes now and tried to avoid seeing outside the plane. She looked at Alexio. That didn't really help, she had to admit.

She said somewhat churlishly, 'I suppose that the likelihood of the plane going down while its owner is on board is not very high.'

He looked smug. 'See?'

Then he leant closer, making her pulse jump out of control.

'And did you know that of all the seats on the plane these are the safest ones to be in—in the event of a crash?'

Sidonie's eyes widened. 'Really?'

She saw humour dancing in those golden depths and clamped her eyes shut again while something swooped precariously in her belly.

'Very funny.'

Then the plane jerked and Sidonie's hands tightened on the armrests. She heard a deep sigh from beside her and then felt her left hand being taken by a much bigger one. Instantly she was short of breath which she could ill afford to lose.

'What are you doing?' she squeaked, very aware of how tiny her hand felt in his.

'If it's all right with you, I'd prefer it if you abused me rather than my armrests.'

Sidonie opened her eyes again and glanced left. Alexio was looking stern, but with a twitch of a smile playing around his mouth. *Lord, oh, Lord.* She said, a little breathlessly, 'I think somehow that your armrests can withstand my feeble attempts to bend them out of shape.'

'Nevertheless,' Alexio replied easily, 'I won't let it be said that I couldn't offer support to a valued customer in her hour of need.'

CHAPTER TWO

SOMETHING HOT AND shivery went through Sidonie's body. He was flirting with her. She felt as if she was teetering on the edge of a huge canyon, with the exhilaration of the fall reaching out to beckon her into the unknown. He was so utterly gorgeous, and so charming when he turned it on. It was smooth, practised. And she was no match for a man like him.

With her body screaming resistance, Sidonie pulled her hand free from his grip and smiled tightly. 'I'll be fine. But, thanks.'

His eyes flashed for a second, as if he were taken aback or surprised. The regret in Sidonie's body was like a sharp pang.

She clasped her hands in her lap, well out of reach, and turned her head, closing her eyes so that she didn't have to look out of the window. Her battle with fear as the plane took off was being eclipsed by her need not to show it to the man beside her.

More than once she wished that he'd take her hand again. His palm had felt ever so slightly callused. The hands of a working man, not a pampered man.

'You can open your eyes now. The seatbelt sign is about to go off.'

Sidonie took a deep breath and opened her eyes, releasing her hands from their death grip on each other. Alexio was looking at her. She had the impression that he'd been looking at her the whole time. She felt clammy. Hot.

He held out his hand then, and said, 'I believe you already know who I am, but I don't know who you are...'

He wasn't backing off. Butterflies erupted in Sidonie's belly again. She couldn't ignore him. She put her hand in his, unable to help a small smile which was only in part to do with the trauma of take-off being over.

'Sidonie Fitzgerald—pleased to meet you.'

He clasped her hand and once again an electric current seemed to thrum through her blood.

'Sidonie...' he mused. 'It sounds French.'

'It is. My mother chose it. I told you she was French.'

'That's right...you did.'

He was still holding her hand and Sidonie felt as if she was overheating. 'Did they just turn the heating up?'

'You do look hot. Maybe you should take your sweat-shirt off.'

He finally released her hand and it tingled. Faintly, Sidonie said, 'I'm sure I'll be fine...' She had no intention of baring herself to this man's far too assessing gaze.

It was then that Sidonie remembered what they'd been talking about. The fact that they'd both lost their mothers recently. That feeling of kinship. Feeling exposed now, she looked away and reached for her book. She held it for a minute and then turned to Alexio again. He had put his head back against the seat, closed his eyes. She felt ridiculously deflated for a moment.

But then she realised she could drink him in unobserved. His profile was patrician. His eyes deep-set, with long dark lashes. His cheekbones would have made a woman weep with envy, but the stark lines of his face took away any pretty edges.

His jaw was firm, even in repose, and she could see the faint stubbling of fresh beard growth. A spasm of lust gripped her between her legs, taking her by surprise. She'd never experienced such raw *desire*. She'd had a couple of boyfriends at college and had had sex, but it had all been a bit…bland. A lot of fuss over nothing. Mildly excruciating. The guys had certainly seemed to enjoy it more than she had.

She could imagine, though, that this man knew exactly what to do…how to make a woman feel exactly as she should. Especially a man with a mouth like his…sensual and wicked. Hard lines but soft contours… Sidonie pressed her legs together to stop the betraying throb between them. She hadn't even known she had a pulse there, but she could feel it now, like a beacon.

'It's rude to stare, you know.'

Sidonie sprang back. Cheeks flaming. One lazy eye had opened and was focused on her, seeing her mortification.

She spluttered, 'How did you know?'

Before she could feel any more embarrassed he bent down and his head of thick dark hair, closely cropped to his skull, came dangerously near to her thighs. Heat bloomed from Sidonie's groin.

Then he straightened up, holding her book in his hand. He took a quick glance at the title before handing it back to her and commenting dryly, '*Techniques for Analysing Successful Business Structures*? That's bound to send you to sleep.'

Sidonie scowled and took the book from him jerkily. 'I'm trying to keep up with my course so that when I go back I won't be too rusty.'

Alexio dipped his head. 'Very commendable.'

Sidonie felt defensive and wasn't even sure why. 'Some of us have to study the subject. We don't have the natural ability or the support to be able to launch a stratospherically successful business first time.'

His mouth tightened and Sidonie knew she'd raised his hackles.

'I didn't have any support—or did your case study not cover that?'

Sidonie flushed and looked down, inspecting a spot of dirt on her jeans. She looked up again. 'I didn't mean it to sound like that… It's common knowledge that you turned your back on your inheritance… However, you can't deny that your background must have given you confidence and an anticipation of success that most mere mortals mightn't feel or experience.'

His face relaxed somewhat and Sidonie felt herself relax too. Weird.

'You're right,' he surprised her by admitting. 'After all, I grew up absorbing my father's business nous whether I want to admit it or not. And I had the best education money could buy… My brother is also a successful entrepreneur, so I learnt from him too.'

Sidonie was itching to ask him why he'd turned his back on his inheritance, but just then the stewardess turned up with a trolley, smiling winsomely at Alexio. Sidonie felt the most bizarre rise of something hot and visceral. Possessiveness. It shocked her so much that she shrank back.

Her sweatshirt felt hot and constricting, even more so now, and Sidonie longed to feel cool. While Alexio was distracted, ordering some coffee from the woman, Sidonie whipped it over her head—only to emerge seconds later to find two pairs of eyes on her. The distinctly cold blue of the stewardess and a green gaze, intent and disturbing.

'What…?' She looked from Alexio to the woman, who now spoke to her in tones even cooler than her arctic gaze.

'Would you like some tea or coffee, madam?'

In fluent French Sidonie replied that she would love some tea. She could sense the small smile playing around Alexio's mouth without even looking. Her skin prickled as she put down her table and accepted the steaming tea. She felt exposed now, in her loose singlet top, even though it was layered over another one.

Before she could reach for her purse Alexio had paid for her drink as well as his. Not a welcome move, according to the pursed lips of the stewardess who moved on with barely disguised huffiness.

Alexio seemed oblivious, though.

'Thank you,' Sidonie said. 'You didn't have to do that.'

He shrugged. 'It's nothing—my pleasure.'

Sidonie shivered a little to think of *his pleasure*.

To get away from such carnal imaginings, she remarked, 'How is it beneficial to do a spot-check on one of your planes if everyone knows who you are?' He quirked a brow at her as he took a sip of coffee and Sidonie blustered a bit. 'Well, you know what I mean. That stewardess will obviously be doing her best to impress.'

'True,' he conceded, and put his cup down.

Sidonie was acutely aware of how dark his hands looked against the cup, how large.

'But I never inform them when I'm coming, and I'm not just interested in the behaviour of my staff—it's everything. I can overhear the passengers' observations too.'

Sidonie frowned. 'But don't you have people who work for you who can do this sort of thing and report back?'

Alexio shrugged minutely. 'I have to go to London today—why not take one of my own commercial flights? If I expect others to do it then I should be able to, too. I am aware of my carbon footprint. I have a responsibility.'

Sidonie could see unimstakable pride in his business on his face. She nodded her head. 'It's smart. Because if anyone ever criticises you you can say that you know first-hand what it's like to fly on your budget flights. And,' she added, warming to her theme, turning more towards

Alexio, 'it gives the customer a sense of kinship with you. You're one of the people.'

He smiled. 'That too. Very good, business student. It's a pity you had to drop out.'

Sidonie glanced away, uncomfortable again under that gaze. It was as if he could see right through her to a place she wasn't even aware of herself. Some secret part she'd not explored yet.

'So your mother was French...and your father?'

Sidonie rolled her eyes and said lightly, 'Back to twenty questions again?'

She sat back and tried not to notice how confined the space was. Their elbows kept touching lightly when they moved. Their thighs would be touching if she shifted hers towards him by about an inch. His legs were so long he had to spread them wide.

Instantly warm again, Sidonie answered before he could comment. 'My father was Irish. My mother went to Dublin many years ago...she met my father and stayed in Dublin and they got married.'

Sidonie slid her gaze from Alexio's, afraid he might see something of her very deep shame revealed. It wasn't exactly the way things had happened, but near enough. He didn't need to know the darker secrets of her parents' relationship and her origins. Or about subsequent shattering events.

She looked at him. 'And you?'

His expression became veiled, piquing her interest.

'My mother was Spanish and my father is Greek. But you probably knew that.'

Sidonie answered, 'I didn't realise your mother was Spanish...'

'I presume your fluent French is from your mother?'

Sidonie nodded and took another sip of tea. She realised

then that if only she wasn't so *aware* of Alexio it would actually be quite nice talking to him.

'She spoke French to me all the time, and my father encouraged it. He knew it would come in handy at some stage.'

'You were close to your father?'

She nodded. 'Why do you ask?'

Alexio reached out and to Sidonie's shock touched her cheek with the backs of his fingers for a fleeting second.

'Because your face softened when you mentioned him.'

Sidonie touched her cheek where he had touched her and felt embarrassed. She ducked her face again, wishing her hair was down so she could hide. 'I loved him. He was a wonderful man.'

'You're lucky to have had that… My father…we don't exactly see eye to eye.'

Sidonie glanced back at him, grateful for the attention to be off her, and laughed slightly. 'Surely he must be one of the proudest fathers in the world?'

Alexio smiled, but it was grim. 'Ah, but my success didn't come through him. I fought for my own piece of the pie and he's never forgiven me for it.'

Just then they were interrupted again, when a different stewardess came along to clear up their rubbish. It gave Alexio a reality check and he balked inwardly.

What on earth was he doing? Blithely spilling his guts to a complete stranger because he was momentarily mesmerised by pale skin, beautiful eyes and a very supple, slim body?

When the stewardess had gone and Alexio was still berating himself he saw Sidonie undo her seatbelt buckle.

She looked at him expectantly before saying, 'I need to go to the bathroom. Please.'

Relieved to have a chance to gather his completely scattered senses, Alexio undid his own seatbelt and stood up. Deliberately he didn't move out into the aisle completely, so that Sidonie had to brush past him. He saw the flash in her eyes, making them sparkle a brilliant blue-green, and felt that punch to his gut again.

As she went past him he saw that she was doing her best not to touch him, but even the most fleeting glance of her hip against his thigh sent shards of desire into his belly. He couldn't help but smell her scent—cool and crisp, with a hint of something floral. That was what she was like— one minute spiky, the next as soft as a fresh rose. And as alluring.

She was taller than he had expected—about five foot seven...

When he'd sat down again, and she'd moved down the aisle to the bathroom, Alexio stuck his head out to watch her, his blood heating through every vein and artery at the way her skinny jeans hugged her slim, shapely legs and cupped her surprisingly lush derriere. To Alexio's consternation he saw more than one other male head dip out to take a look too as she passed.

It felt as if he hadn't taken a proper breath since he'd seen her take off that horrific sweatshirt. He'd happened to look at her for her response when the stewardess had asked if she wanted something, only to find her in the act of taking it off. He'd been unable to look away as Sidonie had fought with the voluminous material, gradually showing tantalising glimpses of pale flesh, slim arms, tiny wrists, delicate shoulders and collarbone.

She'd emerged flushed, and Alexio's libido had been suddenly ravenous. She was wearing a vest top, with a loose singlet over it, so she was showing nothing that wasn't completely respectable. But she might as well have been naked, the effect within Alexio was so violent. He felt like a Victorian man seeing bared arms for the first time; they were almost provocative in their slim, delicately muscled definition.

He'd sat there with a raging erection, trying in vain to concentrate on the conversation and those flashing expressive eyes and not let his gaze drift down to where her small but lush cleavage was revealed under those two tops. The hint of a bright pink bra strap every now and then had enflamed him more than the most expensive lingerie modelled by any of his previous lovers. The memory of his Latin lover of last night was being comprehensively eclipsed.

Alexio wanted to see her—*all of her*—with a hunger that might ordinarily cause him to stop and think. He could already imagine her perfectly formed breasts, made to fit a man's hands like plump fruits. Would her nipples be small and peaked? Or large and succulent? He hadn't been able to resist touching her hot cheek for a second. Her skin was as soft and unblemished as a peach.

This was the kind of desire he'd missed for so long. The kind he'd lamented not feeling last night. Urgent and hot. Utterly compelling. As if he couldn't envisage *not* getting off this plane and taking Sidonie with him so that he could taste her all over. And Alexio had to wonder in that moment if he'd ever really felt like this. Or had it just been a figment of his imagination till now?

The revelation sent him reeling, and he wasn't prepared at all when a soft voice said hesitantly, 'Er…excuse me, Mr Christakos?'

He looked up and there she was, and just like that any semblance of clear-headedness was gone. He was reduced to animal lust again. Her breasts were in his eyeline and he could see the thrust of her nipples against the thin fabric of her two tops, like berries. He had to get up and let her back in, cursing his body, which would not obey his head.

One thing he was sure of as she brushed past him in the small space again and her scent tantalised him: he wanted this Sidonie Fitzgerald with her husky voice with a hunger he'd not known before. And he would have her. Because Alexio Christakos always got what he wanted. Especially women.

Sidonie sat down again and tried to hang on to the control she'd struggled to find in the tiny bathroom space just moments before. She'd splashed cold water on her face, as if that might wake her from the trance she seemed to be in.

Any return of her equilibrium had been short-lived. As soon as she'd got back Alexio Christakos had looked at her—that molten green gaze travelling up from her breasts to her face—and it had been so intense…almost predatory. Her whole body had reacted to it, igniting like a flame. Even the air seemed to be crackling between them now, as if something had been turned up a notch.

He's a playboy, he's a playboy, she repeated like a mantra in her head. *He's programmed to go after anything with a pulse.* But Sidonie grimaced at that. Alexio Christakos, according to her fellow enamoured students, was discerning—only choosing the most stunning models and actresses. The beauties of this era. And Sidonie, with her fair colouring, freckles and wayward hair, did not fall into that category. Not by a long shot. This crazy desire…whatever it was she was feeling…she had to be imagining it.

A wave of mortification rushed up through her body, sending her hot and cold. Was she projecting her own pathetic subconscious fantasies onto this man who had the misfortune to be paired with her for the flight?

She heard him clear his throat beside her and was almost scared to look. She could sense his gaze on her—or could she? With a sick desire to know how badly she'd been deluding herself Sidonie turned her head and met that green gaze head-on. Slamming into it, almost. The breath left her mouth in a little sigh. Her belly swooped and her skin tingled all over. Her nipples drew so tight she could feel them like stinging points, chafing against her lace bra.

'Don't…' he growled softly, intimately. 'Don't call me Mr Christakos again. It makes me feel like an old man. It's Alexio.'

Sidonie could feel the plane dip in altitude. Somehow she found her voice. 'We're landing soon. I won't see you ever again, so it doesn't really matter what I call you.'

'Don't be so sure about that.'

Sidonie blinked. Her heart spasmed in her chest. 'What's that supposed to mean?'

'I'm taking you out to dinner tonight.'

Sidonie had two contradictory reactions. Head and heart/ body. Her heart/body leapt and sizzled. Her head said *Danger! Danger!* He was definitely arrogant, and she was loath to let him see that even a small part of her was tempted. A man like this? He would chew her up over dinner and a one-night stand and then cast her out with little or no second thought.

She was a fleeting interest.

Maybe the lack of air and the confines of economy class had gone to his head. Maybe he was bored, jaded, and something about her intrigued him because she was so different from his usual women.

Sidonie crossed her arms and narrowed her eyes. She saw Alexio's jaw clench, as if he was priming himself for a fight, and something deep within her quivered and then went soft and molten. She fought it. They were both oblivious to the stewardess, who had come to check their seatbelts for landing.

'That sounded remarkably like an order and not an invitation. I'm catching a connecting flight to Dublin—or didn't you hear that part earlier?'

Sidonie wasn't sure exactly why she felt so threatened

by his advance, but she did. Even though she knew she was probably right in her suspicions about why a man like Alexio was flirting with her, a very large part of her wanted to leap into his arms and say *yes*.

She would bet that not many women turned him down— if any. But she wouldn't be able to live with herself if she gave in to him for what she had no doubt would amount to one night. She told herself it was because she valued herself too highly, but she knew, treacherously, that she was afraid of how strongly this man affected her. One night would never be enough. She felt it deep in the pit of her belly. And that freaked her out. She was a naturally responsible and cautious person, not given to spontaneous acts like this.

He cast his glance to the very sexy platinum watch on his wrist, and then back to her. 'I'd say you've missed that connecting flight, and as I'm the owner of the airline company the least you can do is allow me to make it up to you. By taking you for dinner.'

Sidonie snorted inelegantly and quashed the swooping sensation in her belly. 'I don't see you offering everyone on this plane dinner to recompense them for missing their connecting flights.'

That formidable jaw clenched again. 'That's probably because I don't *want* to take them for dinner. However, I would like to take *you* for dinner. *Please*.'

Sidonie's chin lifted, but she quivered inwardly at his *please*. 'I'm a terrible dinner companion. I'm a fussy eater and I'm a vegetarian. Vegan, actually.'

That wasn't true, but some devil inside her was working now. Sparking.

Alexio smiled. 'I'm sure you are a scintillating dinner companion, and I know a fabulous vegetarian restaurant— all the eggplant you can eat.'

That humour danced in his eyes again, transporting him from downright gorgeous to downright irresistible.

Sidonie scowled. He didn't believe her for a second. His eyes dropped down her body and then came back up again. A wickedly sexy slow smile tipped up his mouth, telling her better than any words that dinner and conversation were not the only things on his mind. As if she couldn't feel it vibrating between them. This awareness she'd never felt before.

Sidonie glared at him and tried to will down the heat in her body that mocked her with the realisation that dinner wasn't exactly foremost in *her* mind either. Very belatedly she remembered she had taken off her sweatshirt and scrabbled around to find it and pull it back on.

She heard a sound beside her and looked to see Alexio making a face.

'That thing should be burnt.'

Sidonie gasped, affronted. 'It's my favourite.'

'It's a crime to hide your body underneath that shapeless thing.'

Suddenly there was a sharp thudding and crashing sensation and Sidonie's heart stopped. She felt all her blood drain south.

Instantly Alexio had her hands in his and he was saying soothingly, 'We've just landed, that's all.'

Sidonie's heart was still palpitating. Her ears popped. She could see the ground through the window across the aisle and felt the powerful throttle of the plane as it pulled back.

She looked at Alexio, shocked. 'I've never not noticed landing before.' She'd been distracted. By *him*.

Her hands were still in his and she looked down to see them, so much smaller and paler next to his. As she watched he entwined his fingers with hers and between her legs she throbbed. He exerted pressure on her hands and Sidonie looked up, her head feeling heavy, her blood hot.

For a long, taut moment they just looked at one another. Sidonie's breath grew choppy. Alexio pulled one hand free and brought it up to cup her jaw, his thumb moving back and forth as if learning the shape of her cheek.

His eyes were on her mouth now. She wanted him to kiss her so badly. The air sizzled. And then his eyes met hers again and he emitted a guttural sound like a curse. His jaw clenched. He took his hand away. Sidonie had to bite the inside of her lip to stop herself from crying out.

As if she'd been drugged just by that look Sidonie slowly came back to her senses, and mortification gripped her innards when she realised how she must have looked: like some love-starved groupie.

She jerked back. Thank goodness he hadn't kissed her, because she knew that she would have put up no fight whatsoever. And she hated the part of her that felt *bereft* of the experience. She looked away.

'Sidonie.'

The fact that his voice was rough didn't give her any comfort.

'What?' she snapped, reaching for her bag and putting it on her lap so that she could put her stuff back into it.

She found her glasses and stuck them on, even though she only needed them for reading. They felt like the armour she needed. She looked at him and then wished she hadn't. His face was all stark, lean lines. Nostrils flaring. Eyes dangerous.

People around them were starting to stand up, unbuckling seatbelts, reaching for bags.

Sidonie forgot for a moment that he'd even asked her for dinner. She felt ridiculously vulnerable. Exposed.

'I'm sure you have an assistant waiting nearby to fast-track you off the plane and out of the airport.'

Alexio's mouth firmed. She was right. Even now he could see a uniformed official saying, 'Excuse me...' as he fought his way through the crush to get to Alexio.

He grabbed for her hand and Sidonie glanced around

them, but no one was looking. All eager to get on with their journeys.

'Sidonie, I meant what I said. Come for dinner with me tonight.'

She looked at him and still felt that awful sting of rejection because he hadn't actually kissed her. She hated that it made her feel vulnerable. 'I'm going to Dublin. I can't stay in London just on your...whim.'

His eyes flashed. 'It's not a whim. If you stay I'll take care of you—get you home.'

Sidonie pulled her hand free. She shook her head. 'No... I'm sorry, but I can't.'

The uniformed person was at their seats now and he bent down to say something to Alexio, who made a curt reply. He stood up and reached for his jacket and coat. He looked down at Sidonie, whose eyes had been glued to that magnificent torso as he'd stretched up.

'Come with me. At least let me try to help you make your flight.'

Sidonie looked at him and gulped. Now he was distant, unreadable. A shiver went down her spine and she knew in that moment that she would hate to cross him. He would be a formidable enemy.

Stiffly she said, 'You don't have to do this. I can find my own way and wait for another flight if I have to.'

He sighed deeply. 'Just...don't argue, okay? Come with me—please.'

He held out his hand and Sidonie looked from him to it. This was probably the last time she'd ever see him. On some level she realised with a jolt that she felt as if she could trust this man who was all but a total stranger. Even though she was fighting it.

That revelation stunned her. She'd never trusted easily after the cataclysmic events of her childhood. And losing both parents within such a short space of time, together with the recent revelations about her mother's nefarious actions, had made the world feel increasingly fragile around her. As if nothing she knew was solid any more. Yet being in the company of this man had made Sidonie feel more solid than she'd ever felt. Protected. Which was crazy.

Even more crazy, though, was the fact that Sidonie couldn't resist the lure of a few more minutes with this man. Her hand slipped into his almost of its own volition and it was disconcerting how familiar it felt—and yet how deliciously terrifying, as if she were stepping off a ledge.

She was out of her seat and Alexio was leading her towards the back of the plane, guided by the man who had come to fetch him. The back door was open just for them, with the frosty stewardess saying goodbye, sending Sidonie daggers on seeing her hand clasped tightly in Alexio's.

Hating herself for how much she liked the way her hand felt in his, Sidonie followed him down the steps to where another official and a car were waiting. She heard Alexio give her name to the person and instruct him that her luggage should be brought to meet them on the other side. A VIP customs official inspected her Irish passport.

And then they were in a chauffeur-driven car and speeding towards the terminal Sidonie needed to get to for her connecting flight.

CHAPTER THREE

ALEXIO WAS LOOKING at his smartphone but not seeing any-thing. He was incandescent with rage…and lust. Angry with himself that he'd not taken the opportunity to kiss Sidonie when he'd wanted to. But something had held him back—something that had whispered to him that she wasn't like the women he knew. That the strength of what he was feeling was off the charts.

He prided himself on being a civilised man. With very select tastes. Not a man given to random outbursts or to passionately kissing a woman an hour after meeting her. And yet he'd come within seconds of doing just that.

Yet still…had he let her go? No. He'd all but hauled her off the plane. Sidonie was a tense figure beside him now, her bag on her lap, her hands clasping it.

Unable to help himself, Alexio reached out and touched a finger to her jaw, trailing it over the delicate line. Even that made his body scream with hunger. She tensed even more, but she turned to look at him. Alexio marvelled to himself. One wayward curling strand of hair had come loose and coiled over her shoulder like a burst of silken sunrise. Her cheeks were flushed. No make-up, and those ridiculous black-framed glasses. Her shapeless sweatshirt and those worn jeans. He shouldn't want her. But he did.

He couldn't explain it, but in that moment she was the most beautiful woman he'd ever seen in his life. And suddenly that need was back, even more urgent than before. The realisation hit him: he might never see her again.

Rationality dissolved to be replaced by raw hunger and need. Sidonie obviously saw something on his face, in his eyes, and her own eyes widened, her cheeks getting pinker. Alexio couldn't have stopped himself now if a thousand men had tried to hold him back.

He pulled her into him and slanted his mouth over hers.

That first sweet taste of her soft lips crushed under his made his brain go white with heat. She fell against him, hands pressed to his chest, and Alexio hauled her even closer, his mouth moving over hers, coaxing her to open up to him...

One of his hands moved up her arm to her neck, his thumb angling her chin, cupping her head...and then, after an infinitesimal moment, she opened her mouth on a sigh. He deepened the kiss and all that hunger he'd been holding in exploded in a dizzying rush of desire.

Sidonie was still in shock. Alexio's mouth was on hers, his tongue seeking, thrusting, tasting... She couldn't breathe, couldn't think. And didn't want to. All she knew was that as soon as he'd looked at her so hungrily and then reached for her she'd been ready to throw herself into his arms. The evidence that he did want her was like balm to her ravaged spirit.

There was nothing gentle about his kiss, and she wanted it with every fibre of her being. It was passionate, hotter than anything she'd experienced before. He was tasting and plundering, both hands on her head now, his fingers in her hair, making it loose. Sidonie felt as if she was breaking apart into a million tiny pieces, but it was so delicious...so drugging...that she never wanted it to stop.

A ravenous beast she'd never known before woke inside her and she felt herself matching the passion of Alexio's kiss. Matching it and seeking for more. Now *she* was the one who wanted to taste, nipping at his lower lip with her teeth, feeling the hard resilience of that sensual contour... her tongue automatically soothing where she'd nipped.

She heard a faint sound coming from a long way away. And then Alexio was stopping, pulling back. Sidonie went with him, loath to release him even for a second.

Some sliver of sanity intruded and Sidonie realised that she was clinging to Alexio. And that he'd just been kissing her to distraction in the back of his car. She found the strength to pull herself out of the whirlpool and broke free, breathing harshly. Dazed. Eyes unfocused for a second.

She realised two things at once: the car had come to a halt outside the terminal and it must have been the driver who had made the noise to get their attention.

Alexio's hands were still on her arms, as if she needed support, and his face was still close, those eyes looking heavy-lidded and glittering with all sorts of decadent promises. All she wanted to do was pull him back to her and kiss him again and never stop.

Almost violently she pulled free completely. Her cheeks burned. Her hair was loose and coming down. Quickly she scrabbled with trembling hands to put it back up.

She couldn't look at him. What the hell had just happened? Mutual combustion? And she'd leapt into the fire without a second's hesitation. As much as she'd been a willing participant in what had just happened, it scared Sidonie how quickly she'd lost control.

'We're here,' Alexio said, somewhat redundantly. He was trying to control the clamour of his blood. He felt altered after that kiss. Disorientated.

Sidonie was avoiding his eye, breathing fast. He saw her throat work. She opened her mouth and already he wanted to cover it with his, taste that sweetness again.

There was something so unexpected about her—something that pierced him right through to where he'd never been touched, smashing aside his cynical jaded shell. If he could think for a moment he might even feel suspicious, but right now he was too hot for her to feel anything but carnal hunger.

She glanced at him and all he could see were the swirling blue and green depths of those luminous eyes. She was still wearing those glasses. Then he saw her hand reaching for the door handle, and everything in him rejected the notion that she was going to leave. But before he could stop her she'd looked away, opened the door and was stepping out.

Alexio moved so fast that she was only just straightening up when he reached her side of the car. Her eyes were huge and wary. Someone rushed up with her bag on a trolley and Alexio took it, only just restraining himself from snarling at the completely innocent staff member to leave them alone.

Alexio looked at Sidonie for a long moment, feeling as if he was tipping over a precipice he'd never let himself near before.

'Are you sure I can't change your mind?'

For a second he thought she was about to capitulate, and the blood thundered in his head, but then she bit her lip and shook her head. 'I can't. I need to get back.'

Alexio didn't want to move. 'You have a job?'

She avoided his eye. 'I did… But the restaurant closed down.'

Alexio's body grew tight. 'So there's nothing to rush home for…?' Something very unpalatable occurred to him and he bit out, 'Unless you have a boyfriend?'

Sidonie shook her head quickly and at the same time shot him an insulted look. 'No… I would never do…what we just did…if I had…'

She stopped for a moment, then focused on him again and looked tortured, but it was little comfort to Alexio.

'I just…can't do this. With you.' Her chin lifted. 'I'm not easy, Alexio. I won't just fall into bed with you because you click your fingers and expect me to.'

Alexio wanted to smash aside the trolley, rip off those glasses and grab her, kiss her into submission. Kiss her *again*. Instead he bit out, lying admirably, 'I asked you for dinner, Sidonie, not for sex.'

She blanched and avoided his gaze again, slinging her bag across her body. It did little to douse his desire—the strap coming between her breasts made them stand out, defining their pert shape. *Theos*, what was *wrong* with him? Had he lost all reason in the past hour?

Sidonie took the trolley and said, 'Look…thanks, okay? If I lived in London maybe I'd go out with you, but I don't, and I have to go home.'

She was pulling away, taking the trolley with her case on it, and something like panic gripped Alexio's chest, constricting his breathing. He thrust a hand into his jacket pocket and pulled out a card, handed it to her.

She took it reluctantly and he wanted to push it into her hand, wrap her fingers around it. 'Those are my private numbers. If anything changes…call me.'

After a few torturous seconds she just nodded and said, 'It was nice to meet you…'

And then she pulled the trolley round, disappeared into the departures hall and was swallowed up by a thousand faceless, nameless people.

Alexio did not like this feeling of being out of control. *At all*. It was something he'd fought against his whole life—every time his father had tried to mould him into the son and heir he'd wanted. Every time his father had suffocated him with the weight of his expectations. And most all every time he'd seen his father lose it because he couldn't control his emotions around his cold wife.

And yet this wisp of a woman had managed to slide control out from under his feet without him even noticing.

He cursed volubly.

Twenty minutes later Sidonie was about to scream with frustration. Her body was still sensitive, tingling with an overload of sexual awareness. All she could see in her mind's eye was Alexio Christakos's hard-boned gorgeous face and that mouth-wateringly perfect body, but all she could hear was the airline official saying again, 'Look, miss, I'm sorry. This is the weekend of the England versus Ireland rugby final. There is no way you are going to get a ticket to Dublin today or tomorrow. So unless you want to try swimming the Irish Sea...'

Sidonie felt the press of people behind her, all looking to get home, and felt despair. The official was already dealing with the next person and, despondent, Sidonie turned away. She went back out through the main doors, half expecting to see Alexio still standing there with an imperious look on his face, but he and his car were gone and Sidonie felt absurdly like crying.

Why had she been so hell-bent on denying herself an evening with the most charismatic man she'd ever met? The ghost of her mother whispered to her, reminding Sidonie of her strong instinct to deny anything that was just for herself. She always had to work for it.

She'd vowed long ago not to be grasping like her mother, who had been oblivious to the pain of others around her—especially that of her husband, who had devoted his life to her in spite of the fact that she'd humiliated him publicly. In spite of the fact that he'd always known that Sidonie wasn't even his biological daughter.

And now she had a huge responsibility: Tante Josephine

needed her support. She didn't have the luxury of just thinking about herself. A small voice taunted her. *But you could have had tonight. One night.*

Sidonie felt a lurch as she thought of how for one second she'd almost given in to Alexio and said *yes* when he'd asked if she would change her mind.

The one thing that should have held her back was her aunt—but she had gone on her annual two-week holiday with a local charity group. Sidonie had encouraged her to go, knowing it would take her aunt's mind off things while she sorted herself out in Dublin. For an exhilarating second Sidonie had remembered this and thought it might be possible…but she hadn't seized the moment. Too afraid to throw caution to the wind and trust completely.

And it was too late now anyway. She looked down and saw her hand clenched around his card. Her belly flipped. She had an image of him on his way into London to his important meeting. He would have forgotten about her already. An aberration. She'd missed her chance. Maybe she'd even dreamt him up?

A hollow feeling made her ache inside. She turned around again and faced the door, steeling herself to go back into that throng. She would buy a seat on the next available flight and then she would find somewhere to stay—

'Sidonie.'

Her heart slammed to a stop and the blood rushed from her head to her feet. *It couldn't be.*

Sidonie forgot about the trolley and whirled around. Alexio was standing there, as gorgeous as she remembered. Not a dream. Shock mixed with relief and joy jumped in her belly.

'What are you doing here? You were gone,' she breathed, half afraid she was hallucinating.

Alexio's mouth tightened as if he didn't like admitting it. 'I doubled back…just in case.'

Sidonie made a gesture behind her. 'All the flights are full. A rugby match is on between England and Ireland. I can't get home till the day after tomorrow at the earliest...'

'So you're stuck here at the airport? That's unfortunate.' His eyes were glinting with that dark humour again.

Incredible joy was bubbling up inside Sidonie. He'd come back. *For her*. He hadn't forgotten about her.

She fought back the goofy grin threatening to erupt. 'I was going to rebook my flight and then I was going to find somewhere to stay.'

Alexio put one hand in the pocket of his trousers. His jacket hung open. He was stunning, blinding. Mesmerising.

'I happen to have a very spacious apartment here in London. If you were to agree to accompany me to dinner this evening I'd let you stay. And then I'd make sure you got home at the earliest opportunity.'

Warning bells went off in Sidonie's head again but she ignored them. She was getting a second chance. She'd never thought she'd see this man again, because she would never have had the nerve to call him.

She made a mental decision and took a step into the terrifying and exhilarating unknown.

'I'll accept your offer.'

Something within her leapt to see his eyes flare and his cheeks darken with colour.

She held up a hand. 'On one condition.'

'What?' he bit out, clearly impatient now.

'That you allow *me* to buy dinner...for letting me stay with you.'

Sidonie had a mental image of her bank account and her already close to maxed-out credit card after the flights she'd had to take back and forth to Paris in recent months. She bit her lip.

'Except I hope you like cheap Italian, because that's about the best I can offer.'

Alexio stepped up to her and reached around to get her trolley, taking her small case off it as if it weighed nothing. He took her elbow in his hand and looked down at her, taking her breath away.

'I'll tell you what. We'll eat in—that way we don't have to worry about who's paying.'

'But...' Sidonie spluttered ineffectually as he handed her into the back seat of his car.

He came around and got in the other side and then just looked at her, and it was so stern that she stopped.

'Okay—fine. I get it,' she said a little mutinously, 'but I just don't want you to think that I'm not grateful.'

Alexio issued a terse command in a guttural language and Sidonie saw the car's privacy window slide up silently. Then he was reaching for her and pulling her sweatshirt up and over her head before she had the wits to stop him. When she emerged he had his hands in her hair, taking it out of its confines and making it fall down around her shoulders.

Then he plucked off her glasses—which weren't doing much for her sight anyway.

She slapped at his hands ineffectually. 'What do you think you're doing?'

Sidonie hated that her whole body sizzled at his masterful actions, knowing she should be objecting vociferously.

He took her face in his hands, holding her still. Sidonie's heart skipped and her breath stopped.

'Much better,' Alexio breathed approvingly, just before his head bent and his mouth met hers.

Sidonie groaned deeply, because from the moment she'd pulled away from that first kiss she'd craved this again. In her mind she ordered herself to stop thinking and gave herself up to the dark fantasy of Alexio Christakos, who had just turned her world upside down and inside out.

By the time they pulled up outside a huge, impressive building Sidonie felt completely flustered, aching and undone. Alexio's tie was loose and he looked as feverish as Sidonie felt.

'Come in with me. Wait for me.'

Sidonie's mouth felt swollen. She wasn't sure if her vocal cords worked any more. She just nodded her head. It was as if in the space of the back of that car, in the space of the increasingly passionate kisses they'd shared, some indelible link had been forged between them. She was loath to let him out of her sight.

He held her hand walking in, but Sidonie caught sight of her reflection and balked. She jerked in his grip and he looked down at her and raised a brow.

Sidonie blushed. 'I don't look exactly *corporate*.'

His hot gaze swept her up and down and he said throatily, 'You look perfect.'

But Sidonie knew she was out of place in her chain-store tops, jeans and sneakers the moment the immaculate blonde receptionist sent her a look that could have frozen the Sahara.

When they emerged from the lift there was a veritable entourage of people waiting for Alexio. Someone took his jacket and coat; someone else handed him a folder. Someone else was on the phone. And then someone approached her and said, solicitously, 'Miss Fitzgerald? If you'd like to follow me I can show you where you can wait…'

Sidonie was looking helplessly at Alexio, who glanced at her and then waved her off in the direction of her guide. He was already being spirited away in the opposite direction.

Sidonie was led down plush carpeted hallways. She saw the distinctive Christakos logo on the walls and blanched when she realised that this entire building must be *his*.

The young woman in a pristine trouser suit with her dark hair clipped back showed Sidonie into a palatial office with huge windows looking out over what seemed to be the whole of London. This had to be Alexio's office, with its massive desk near the window.

The woman spoke with an accent that Sidonie guessed must be Greek. 'Can I get you anything, Miss Fitzgerald?'

Sidonie looked at her and felt even more mussed up. 'Er...maybe some tea would be nice?'

'Of course. I'll be right back.' And she left and pulled the heavy door behind her.

Alexio's scent was in the air, faint and tantalising. Exclusive. Masculine. *Sexy.* Sidonie took a deep breath in and walked over to the window to take in the view. It was spectacular, breathtaking.

She could see doors leading out to a terrace and opened them. She went out and was confronted with the real vista—not behind a plane of glass. It was in that moment that she had the full, gut-churning sense of the man she'd met only a few short hours before. He was one of the kings of the world.

'Miss Fitzgerald?'

Sidonie whirled around to see the assistant hovering with a tray. She rushed forward, aghast, and took the tray from the startled woman. 'I can look after it myself. Thank you so much.'

The woman backed away. 'If you need anything else I'm just down the hall. Mr Christakos shouldn't be too long, I heard him say he wanted to keep the meeting short.'

Sidonie's belly somersaulted. Was that because of *her*? She nodded her head and the woman left. Sidonie put down the tray. She didn't want to sit at Alexio's desk so she sat at a small coffee table on the other side of the room. She noticed that her hand was trembling when she poured the tea.

Lord. What was she *doing* here? Sitting in Alexio Christakos's palatial office, waiting for him. He'd picked her up on a *plane*.

Sidonie blushed. She'd engaged him in conversation in

the first place. If she'd buried her head in her book he probably wouldn't have looked twice at her. Sidonie put down her teacup. She knew she could walk out of there right now, get her bag out of his car and melt into the crowds in London and quite possibly never see Alexio again… But, treacherously, she didn't want to.

The novel sensation of putting herself first was uncomfortable. It felt like a coat she'd never worn. Tante Josephine's face popped into her mind…but even Tante Josephine was okay for the moment, on holiday with her friends. There was no reason why Sidonie couldn't be here, doing this.

Sidonie felt a sense of lightness, freedom, and it was heady. Dinner tonight. A place to stay. A chance to get to know this amazing man a little better. She breathed deeply and tried to quell her rapid heartbeat. That was all. And that was all she wanted. No matter what her body might be screaming for. She would emerge from this adventure with her emotions intact.

When Alexio could finally get away from his meeting, which he'd cut ruthlessly and uncharacteristically short, he headed for his office, pulling at his tie impatiently as he did so. *Sidonie*. When he'd ordered his driver to turn around before they'd hit the main motorway into London he'd felt like an abject fool. But the compulsion to go back and see her again had been too great. To find her, persuade her to stay.

And then she'd been standing there, like a lost waif, looking at his card, and the sheer relief that had rushed through him had eclipsed any niggling concerns about his uncharacteristic behaviour.

And now she was here, waiting for him. Alexio gritted his jaw to stop his body reacting. He had to get it together. It had been hard enough to concentrate in the meeting.

When he went into his office he didn't see her and his blood turned to ice.

She'd left.

But then he saw the open terrace doors and his heart started beating again. He went forward and saw her slimly curvaceous form, that plump bottom, as she leant against the railing, taking in the view.

He went right up behind her and put his arms next to hers on the railing.

She started for a moment. 'You scared me.'

Alexio imagined that he felt her heart pick up pace— or was it his? Her lush derriere pressed against him *right there*. And Alexio didn't have a hope in hell of controlling his body.

She was tense in the circle of his arms. 'Your meeting wasn't very long.'

Alexio put out his hand and pulled her long, rippling hair over one shoulder, baring her neck. It was a crime to confine such hair. He bent his head and pressed his mouth to the soft skin just under her ear. Immediately she quivered and her bottom moved against him. His other arm came down and wrapped around her midriff, dragging her in tighter.

Theos. He would take her right here and now if he could.

He drew back slightly, dragging in breath, control. 'I told them I had urgent business to attend to.'

Sidonie turned around in his arms and that was worse— because now Alexio's steel-hard erection was pressed against her soft belly and the hard tips of her breasts were visible through her sleeveless vest tops.

'Alexio...'

Alexio dragged his gaze up and met two pools of aqua-marine.

'Hmm?'

'If I stay with you tonight...that doesn't mean I'm going

to sleep with you…' She bit her lip. 'I'm not saying I don't want to, but I'm not like that.' She winced. 'I mean…I won't sleep with you as some sort of payment. I would prefer to stay in a hostel or something.'

Alexio cupped her jaw. She *would* sleep with him. They both knew it.

'I think you've already made your morals clear, and I respect that. Firstly, you are *not* staying in a hostel or anywhere else.' His voice was rough. 'Secondly, I do not expect you to sleep with me to pay me for the room. *If* you sleep with me it will be because you want to. Not for any other reason. We're two consenting adults, Sidonie, not bound by any ties. Free to do as we wish…'

She was breathless now. He could feel her chest moving against him and he wanted to groan.

'Yes…but after tonight we won't see each other again… I don't do one-night stands. We barely know each other.'

Alexio bent his head and feathered a kiss at the corner of one succulent pouting lip. He could feel her yielding against him.

'I already know more about you than I do about my own secretary. And I thought you said you couldn't get a flight for at least a couple of days…so that's two nights… And you know what? You think too much. Tomorrow is a long way away. We have tonight, and that's all that matters right now.'

Alexio's apartment was not as Sidonie had expected. She'd anticipated some kind of penthouse apartment in a sleek building, but his loft-style apartment was in an old converted redbrick building on the Thames, with stunning views.

It had huge windows and exposed brick walls. Sleek and modern furnishings married well with the old shell of the building. Abstract art and compelling black and white photos hung on the walls. The furnishings were unmistakably masculine, but not in an off-putting way. It was comfortable.

Alexio was standing with his arms crossed, watching her. Sidonie blushed and answered his look. She shrugged slightly. 'I'd expected something a bit more...'

'Generic? Without taste?' Alexio put a hand to his chest. 'You wound me...although maybe when you see this your suspicions will be proved right.'

He took her hand and led her to an alcove off the main open-plan living area. It was a dark nook, decorated like an opulent private gentlemen's club, with a pool table and a fully stocked antique bar. A huge mirror behind the bar made the whole space glitter with decadence.

Sidonie smiled. 'Now, this is more like it.'

Alexio let her go and moved to the bar. He disappeared behind the counter to re-emerge holding a chilled bottle of champagne and two glasses.

Sidonie's skin prickled.

He arched a brow. 'Can I tempt you with an aperitif?'

Sidonie saw then how the light was lengthening outside the huge stunning windows and over London. London Bridge was in view—an iconic landmark. She hadn't even noticed that the day had almost flown by.

Vowing to stop thinking so much and just to enjoy, she went and perched herself on one of the velvet-covered stools.

'I'd love one, thank you.'

Alexio expertly popped the cork with only the smallest, most sibilant hiss, and poured them both a glass of the sparkling golden liquid. Sidonie tried not to notice the label, which proclaimed it to be one of the most expensive brands in the world.

Don't think. Enjoy.

He handed her a glass and then came around the counter to stand in front of her. If she widened her legs Alexio could step right between them. Sidonie's pulse leapt.

But he merely clinked his glass to hers and said, 'To us, Sidonie Fitzgerald. Thank you for coming with me today.'

Sidonie couldn't look away from that green gaze. 'Cheers…and thank you for your hospitality.'

They both took a sip and Sidonie blinked at the effervescent bubbles rushing down her throat. She felt buoyed up, heady. Alexio took her hand again and something within her loved the way he did it.

He tugged her gently from the stool. 'Let me give you the tour.'

Carrying their glasses, Alexio brought her through the living area and showed her the sleek kitchen, which again had a lived-in look about it.

'Do you cook?' she asked curiously.

He shrugged minutely. 'I can cook enough for me. I wouldn't put it to the test of a dinner party, though.'

Sidonie teased him to hide her nervousness. 'So what have you lined up for tonight? Beans on toast?'

He looked back at her. 'A chef from one of London's best restaurants. He'll be arriving to serve us in about an hour.'

'Oh…' That shut Sidonie up. For a second she'd almost forgotten who she was with…

Alexio was leading her up some wooden stairs now, with brass railing banisters. There was glass everywhere, all the spaces blending into one another seamlessly as only the best architecture could.

This upper level was like a mezzanine. Alexio was leading her to a room on the left, and Sidonie could see her bag on a huge white-covered bed. A window looked out over the Thames, and the *en suite* bathroom was rustic and yet delightfully modern, with two sinks and an enormous wet-room-style shower. A huge antique bath stood alone.

'It's gorgeous,' she breathed, her hand tightening unconsciously around Alexio's fingers.

He exerted pressure back and she looked at him.

'This is your room, Sidonie. Like I said, I don't expect you to sleep with me…but I won't deny that I want you.'

Just that. Stark. No games. No false seduction. He wanted her. It was devastating in its simplicity.

Feeling shaky, Sidonie just replied, 'Okay…thank you…'

Before they left he showed her how to pull the huge white curtains across the windows that were both walls and door for privacy.

Then he was leading her out along the corridor to another room. This one had to be his. Much larger. Bare but for some choice furniture. An enormous bed, a chair, a wardrobe and a chest of drawers. And again that amazing view.

His *en suite* bathroom was black-tiled, undeniably masculine.

They came back out and Alexio showed her two other guest rooms and an office that looked to be equipped with enough technology to make a space rocket take off.

'London is my next main base after Athens,' he explained. 'I spend most of my time between here and there.'

He led her back down to the bar and Sidonie perched on the stool again. Alexio refilled her glass and then produced a bowl of fresh strawberries from somewhere. Sidonie almost groaned when he dipped one in champagne and handed it to her. The taste of the sweetly tart fruit exploded in her mouth. She wasn't unaware of his intent look at her mouth and she melted inside. She knew that at some point she would have to make things very clear to herself about how far she was prepared to go, because Alexio was waiting for the barest sign of encouragement. And yet she believed him when he said he'd leave it up to her. He wouldn't put pressure on her. He wouldn't have to!

Speaking of inconsequential things as the light outside Alexio's apartment faded into dusk, Sidonie felt herself being more and more seduced. That line she didn't want to cross was blurring and becoming something she wanted to leap over. The sparkling wine did little to help her keep her inhibitions raised.

After a while Alexio glanced at his watch and made a face. 'I don't know about you but I'd like to freshen up— and the chef will be here soon.'

Immediately he said that Sidonie felt sticky after the long day. She nodded. 'I'd love to have a shower…if that's okay.'

Alexio looked at her, and she was shocked and thrilled at the explicitness of it.

'Meet you back down here in twenty minutes?'

'Okay.' Sidonie slid off the stool.

She relished the opportunity to get some space, even for a few minutes. Alexio was so all-encompassing. She still couldn't really believe she was here, with him.

When she let herself into her bedroom she pulled the drapes over the door and windows, marvelling again at the genius design. She went to the main windows overlooking the view and opened one, breathing in the late spring London air.

London Bridge was teeming with traffic, but Sidonie felt deliciously cut off from everything. The real world was fading, being held at bay. With Tante Josephine safe, and away from her own worries, Sidonie could fool herself into thinking she had no responsibilities. She could just…*indulge*.

Realising that she was standing mooning at the view, she galvanised herself into action, unpacked some things and took her shower.

Afterwards, wrapped in a towel, she bit her lip as she looked at her pathetic clothes options. Jeans and more jeans. T-shirts. She had one smart outfit that she'd brought over for the meeting with the solicitor, but that was a black skirt she'd worn for work as a waitress and a black shirt. She'd look as if she was going to a funeral.

Clothes had become a luxury a long time ago, when she'd sold most of her more expensive items to help pay for college while her father had been struggling.

She felt absurdly gauche right then, knowing that Alexio must be used to women who dressed like...*women*. Not impoverished students. Which was what she was. But what she wouldn't give right now for some sleek little black number...

Sighing deeply, Sidonie reached for a pair of dark denims that might be construed as smart and selected a grey T-shirt with a glittery sequin design on the shoulders. She slipped on the slingback heels she'd worn for the meeting and, after inspecting herself in the mirror and balking at her freshly scrubbed pink face, applied some make-up to try and make up for her woefully inappropriate outfit.

She was tempted to put her hair up again, but recalled Alexio taking it down earlier. The thought of those hands and long fingers touching her made her leave it alone. She didn't want to tempt him in any way unless she was competely prepared for his response. But then, she didn't think she'd ever be prepared for the response of a man like Alexio.

Sidonie took a deep breath, as if that might ease the tumult in her breast and in her blood. The ease with which this relative stranger seemed to have sneaked under her skin scared her and exhilarated her in equal measure. It was like being on a rollercoaster ride with no one at the controls.

CHAPTER FOUR

ALEXIO CAUGHT A movement out of the corner of his eye and looked up from where he was pouring some wine into two glasses. His heart stopped in his chest.

Sidonie stood at the bottom of the stairs, her hands clasped together. She was in black figure-hugging denims and pointy shoes. She wore a grey T-shirt with something that sparkled on its shoulders. She hadn't put her hair up—*because she knew he'd just take it down?*—and it tumbled over her shoulders, glowing with an inner fire that flared under certain lights.

Despite the obvious cheapness of her clothes, once again he was struck by her natural beauty, and he wondered how on earth he'd ever dismissed her. The jeans he'd put on felt restrictive, and he gritted his jaw against his newly rampant libido. He had been mourning its dysfunction only twenty-four hours ago. The irony was not lost on him.

He put down the wine bottle and walked over. He saw her cheeks flush as he got nearer. His blood leapt in response. It was as if they were linked. Attuned to exactly the same rhythms. Making love with this woman… Alexio knew instinctively that one night would not be enough, but he pushed that revelation down rather than deal with the skin-prickling awareness of something dangerous that accompanied it.

She looked nervous and gestured to her clothes, clearly

self-conscious, making Alexio feel as if he wanted to re-assure her in a way that no other woman of his acquaintance ever needed.

'I didn't come prepared for a fancy dinner. You'll have to excuse me.'

Alexio took her hand. His voice was gruff. 'I want you to be comfortable. I didn't make much effort either.'

He saw her eyes drop to take in his plain white shirt and faded jeans. Bare feet. She looked back up again and her eyes had grown wider, their pupils dilated. Her cheeks were more flushed. *She wanted him*.

She obviously heard movement in the kitchen and said, 'Was I longer than twenty minutes?'

He smiled. 'About forty…but I allowed for that. It seems a safe bet where a woman is concerned.'

He immediately saw the aquamarine fire in her eyes, the way her small chin tipped up, and expected a tart reply. But he wouldn't let her hand go when she tried to pull away. He had to keep touching her. It was like a compulsive need.

'You've known a lot of women, then, to make this empirical study of their time-keeping on a general level?'

Alexio's smile faded. He could see past the bluster to where there was a hint of genuine insecurity. He touched her jaw and saw her mouth firm, as if warding off his effect on her.

'I'm no monk, *glikia mou*. But neither am I half as promiscuous as the press would like to paint me. When I take lovers I'm always up front. I don't offer anything more than mutual satisfaction. I'm not into relationships right now.'

Sidonie looked at him with that incredibly direct gaze that seemed to sear straight through him.

'Okay…' she said, and smiled, showing that gap between her teeth.

Alexio wanted to throw her over his shoulder so that he could take her upstairs right now and to hell with dinner.

She grinned then in earnest, and bent down to do something. Alexio saw her shoes being kicked off on the floor and her height dropped by an inch.

'Well, seeing as you're not making an effort to wear shoes,' she clarified, 'I don't see why I have to go through the pain.'

Before he did something to inadvertently demonstrate how off-centre she made him feel, Alexio tugged her towards the dining area, where a table had been laid for two, complete with lit candles. It was by the window, with a view of London lit up by night beyond the river and the bridge.

The chef's assistant was setting out their starters and Alexio said, 'Thanks, Jonathan. I think we can take it from here. Say thank you to Michel for me.'

The young man exited swiftly.

Alexio had done this many times before—for business meals in his apartment as well as for women—but tonight it felt different. Sidonie was looking at everything with such wide eyes.

'I presumed you were joking earlier about being a vegetarian.'

Alexio lifted the platter's lid to reveal *confit* duck dumplings and saw Sidonie's eyes gleam with anticipation. It had a direct effect on his body, and he wondered if she would have that same hungry look when they made love.

She had the grace to glance at him sheepishly. 'I had you figured for a chest-beating carnivore who would be horrified at the thought of watching me chew a lettuce leaf for half an hour.'

Alexio held Sidonie's chair out for her so she could sit down, and said in a low, throaty voice as she did so, 'I had a vegetarian option lined up just in case…but don't you know by now that nothing you could have said would have put me off?'

He was rewarded by pink cheeks when he took his own

seat opposite her. He raised his glass of white wine and she took hers. *'Yiamas.'*

Sidonie repeated the Greek phrase. They both took a sip of their drinks and Alexio dished out the starter.

'Don't you know by now that nothing you could have said would have put me off?' Alexio's softly delivered words still echoed in Sidonie's head. The steel behind them…

He had just taken their dessert plates into the kitchen and Sidonie was standing on the small terrace which hugged the side of the building, leaning on the railing, with the Thames moving beneath her feet somewhere in the dark.

In all honesty she couldn't have recalled, if asked, what they'd just eaten except to know that it had been exquisite. She'd been too mesmerised by her charismatic dinner companion and how easily the conversation had flowed. Like on the plane, once they'd started they hadn't stopped. Every now and then a tiny jolt of electric shock had run through her at the realisation of where she was and with whom… She'd met him only hours before… She should be back in Dublin, reorganising her life…

She still wanted to cringe when she thought of the way Alexio had looked her up and down when she'd arrived downstairs in her jeans and T-shirt, acutely conscious of how tatty she must look. The fact that he was equally dressed down had been little comfort, because she'd almost melted on the spot at seeing him in the faded hip-hugging jeans and white shirt. He epitomised cool, laid-back elegance.

To give him credit, he hadn't made her feel uncomfortable. Just hot and bothered…

She heard a noise in the kitchen and turned round to see Alexio putting plates in a dishwasher. She shook her head wryly. Who would have believed it?

She walked back in to help. He stood up tall.

'Coffee? An after-dinner liqueur?'

Sidonie put the last plate in the dishwasher and closed the door. She'd made a decision during dinner—a momentous one. It had been helped by the direct way he'd informed her earlier that he wasn't *'into relationships'*. Well, neither was she. Not when she faced such a huge upheaval in her life, and not when she had responsibilities. And certainly not when the man was Alexio Christakos and so far out of her league it wasn't funny.

During dinner Sidonie had recalled the name of a favourite perfume of her mother's: *Ce Soir ou Jamais*. Tonight or never. This evening felt all too ephemeral. She wanted to seize the moment, live it fully. She wanted this man with a hunger she knew was rare. Once in a lifetime.

She turned and put her hands behind her against the counter and looked up. *Was she really going to do this?* Her sex spasmed in response. *Yes.* She wanted one night with this man, just one night of decadent escapism, and then she would walk away knowing what it was like to be truly made love to.

Having no idea how to go about letting a man like Alexio know what she wanted, without declaring baldly that she wanted to have sex with him, Sidonie seized on an idea. 'I'd like a liqueur, please…and did I mention that I'm a mean pool-player?'

Alexio went still and shook his head. 'No, you did not. I believe we touched on many subjects over dinner, including favourite films and music, and you tried to trick me into telling you the secrets of my success, but there was no mention of your pool abilities.'

Sidonie bit back a grin. And a sigh. This man should come with a warning label: *Approach with caution! You are liable to get burnt if you stand too close.* It was too late for her. She would burn for ever in the tormenting hell of regret if she didn't allow herself to indulge in this fantasy.

'Well, I happened to be something of a local champion in college. And I would like to challenge you to a game, Mr Christakos.'

Alexio leant back against the opposite counter and crossed his arms. 'Interesting, Miss Fitzgerald. Tell me… are there terms for this challenge?'

Sidonie crossed her arms too and tried to look mock serious—not as far out of her depth as she felt. 'Of course. My terms are simple: whoever wins gets to decide what we do for the rest of the night.'

Sidonie's heart was beating so hard now she felt light-headed. Alexio looked serious, but his eyes had darkened.

'I take it that if you win your choice will be…?'

Sidonie affected an air of piety. 'To go to bed with a good book, of course.'

His eyes flashed. 'And if I win…and I ask you nicely to come to bed with me…?'

Sidonie shrugged minutely. 'Then I guess I'll have to suffer the consequences.' She straightened up and dropped her arms. 'But you won't win, so maybe I should just leave now…'

She made to walk off and like lightning Alexio grabbed her hand and hauled her into him. Sidonie gasped. His body was hard all over, pressed against hers. Her legs promptly turned to jelly.

'Not so fast.' His voice was low, seductive. 'I believe you challenged me to a game, and in light of the fact that I'm doomed to failure I'd like to raise the stakes a little… For every shot lost, we also lose a piece of clothing.'

Sidonie's blood rushed to her every erogenous zone at the thought of seeing Alexio bared. 'There's no such game,' she said breathlessly as Alexio pulled her in the direction of the bar and games room.

'There is now, sweetheart.'

Alexio let Sidonie go when they got into the darkened

room. After he had poured them both drinks—a liqueur for her and a whisky for him—he took out two cues and handed her one. Sidonie made a big show of chalking it up while Alexio put out the balls.

When they were laid out he flourished an arm. 'Please, ladies first.'

Sidonie moved around the table, deliciously aware of Alexio's eyes on her, and yet still a little terrified. She wasn't sure what demon had made her come up with this idea—as if she thought she could make it look as if her decision *wasn't* fuelled with the desperate need she really felt. As if she played these kinds of games with men all the time.

Eventually she settled on a point to start and positioned herself, drawing back the cue. She was on the opposite side of the room to Alexio and he sat with his hip was hitched against a stool, his legs long, thighs powerful underneath the denim. Distracting her already.

'Take as long as you like,' he said, in a patronising tone which enflamed Sidonie enough for her to scatter the balls masterfully, potting her first one.

She stood up and smiled. 'You were saying…?'

Alexio scowled. 'Beginner's luck.'

Sidonie walked around the table again, aware of the tension in the small room thickening. As she took her next shot she realised too late that her palms were sweaty and the cue slipped slightly, throwing her off and making her lose her aim. She missed.

Alexio tsked and stood up. Sidonie's heart thumped hard. *For every shot lost, we also lose a piece of clothing.* Alexio smiled and it was the smile of the devil.

'I don't mind what goes, but I'd suggest your T-shirt or your trousers.'

Now Sidonie scowled. She'd thought she'd have a little more time. She'd also thought she'd have him almost naked before her, giving her time to get used to it. Then she thought of something and smiled sweetly, executing a nimble move so that she undid her bra, pulled its strap down one arm and then pulled it out neatly from the armhole of her T-shirt. An old boarding school trick.

Alexio's face darkened ominously. 'That's cheating.'

Sidonie grinned. 'Not at all. I took your suggestion on board and ignored it.'

She tossed her bright pink bra onto the seat beside her and saw Alexio's eyes follow the movement and then come back to linger on her braless chest. Her breasts felt tight and heavy, their tips pushing against the cotton of her top. Alexio's cheeks flushed and it had a direct effect on the pulse in her groin.

Slowly he put down his drink and stood up. Sidonie crossed her arms and then quickly thought better of it when Alexio's eyes widened and she realised she was only making things worse.

He took his eyes off her with visible effort. Despite all their play, Sidonie's blood was infused with a heady feminine energy at having this man look at her with such naked desire. But she got distracted when he came close and bent over the pool table right in front of her, and her eye was drawn helplessly to his taut, muscular buttocks.

She couldn't see exactly what he was doing, but he'd hit the ball and nothing was pocketed.

He turned around and said, 'Whoops…' and started undoing his shirt.

Sidonie's mouth went dry at seeing his torso revealed bit by bit. And when he shrugged the shirt off completely she went weak at the knees.

He was stunning. Beautifully muscled. Not an ounce of fat. Broad and powerful. Very masculine whorls of hair dusted his chest, leading down to that tantalising line which disappeared into his jeans. They clung precariously to his hips and Sidonie had to clench her hands to fists to stop herself reaching out to undo that top button. She gulped when she saw the bulge pushing insistently against the denim.

His rough voice cut through the heat in her brain. 'Your turn, I think.'

He turned to walk away and Sidonie felt as if someone had just hit her. His back was as beautiful as his front. Wide and smooth. He turned around at the bar and leant on it nonchalantly, arched a brow.

Sidonie forced herself to move and looked at the table. She couldn't seem to compute what to do any more. She hadn't been boasting—she knew she could play and quite possibly beat Alexio on a good day. But right now…she was useless. Eventually she saw the shot she needed to take. But she couldn't get that torso out of her mind, those muscles rippling under silken flesh. *Hard*.

Predictably, Sidonie missed the shot—because just as she moved so did Alexio. She stood up and glared across at him, feeling hot. 'Now, *that's* cheating.'

He arched a brow, all innocence wrapped up in the devil—*again*. 'I don't know what you're talking about…'

And then his look changed to one so carnal her toes curled.

'Shirt or trousers, Sidonie—unless you've got some very cute way to take off your panties from under your jeans without removing them.'

Of course she didn't. Sidonie huffed. She only had one choice, really. She wasn't about to bare herself completely to the sexiest man she'd ever met. So off came the jeans. She wriggled out of them, deliberately avoiding his gaze, self-conscious in her very plain white panties decorated with flowers.

Alexio watched with a heavy-lidded gaze as Sidonie carefully folded her jeans and put them to the side, near the bright pink splash of her bra. The same pink bra that had been tantalising him all day. The way she folded her jeans made him feel weak inside. There was something curiously vulnerable about it.

Now she looked at him, and her chin was up. *Brave.* She wasn't half as confident as she was letting on. Alexio hid the way that made him feel by focusing on her gently swaying breasts beneath her T-shirt. They were beautifully rounded and pert. Their tips hard. His mouth watered. His erection got harder. He had to shift on the stool.

Her hips were slim, but womanly. Her panties looked positively virginal with their cute flowers. Yet the way she was looking at him now as he caught her gaze again was anything but virginal. *Good.* Because when they came together Alexio knew he wouldn't have the patience to go slowly.

Aware that he couldn't actually stand up without revealing how turned on he was, Alexio said, 'I'm feeling generous. You can have another shot.'

Sidonie looked determined this time. 'That's the last piece of clothing I'll be removing.'

She picked up the cue and moved around the table again, clad only in her T-shirt and panties. The soft white cotton hugged her bottom, revealed in all its lushness now.

Alexio had to admit that his jaded palate was well and truly *un*jaded now. He'd never been so turned on in his life. He'd never been brought so close to the edge without even touching a woman before.

And then Sidonie stopped right in front of him, her back to him. He saw a sliver of pale skin, the gentle curve of her lower back just over the band of her panties. He saw the two dimples of Venus above her buttocks and nearly groaned out loud.

When she bent over the table and widened her legs to get a better aim the tiny thread holding his control together snapped completely. With a feral sound Alexio wrapped an arm around her bare midriff and deftly scooped Sidonie back against him, ignoring her soft squeal of surprise. He took the cue out of her hands, throwing it to one side.

She was breathing heavily. 'That's not fair. That's blatantly against the rules. Obstruction.'

'Damn the rules,' Alexio growled, turning Sidonie around to face him. Her eyes were dark blue now, the pupils huge.

'You win. I forfeit the game,' he said.

Sidonie couldn't hide the crestfallen expression on her face as she obviously considered for a second that she had been hoist by her own petard. Alexio wanted to howl in triumph, but he played it out.

'So I guess this means you're going to bed with a book then?'

Sidonie looked sheepish. 'I don't have one with me apart from my textbook.'

Alexio made a face. 'Too bad…maybe I can change your mind?'

'How are you going to do that?'

Sidonie's breath was getting choppier. Her breasts under their thin cotton covering were teasing his bare skin now, making him harder.

'Like this…'

Alexio picked her up and sat her on the edge of the pool table, then came to stand between her spread legs. He cupped her face and her jaw in his hands and did what he'd been aching to do all evening: he covered her mouth with his and sank into dark, sweet, urgent oblivion.

Sidonie clutched Alexio's wide shoulders, her fingers digging into smooth hot skin. The question had been asked and answered. He knew she wanted this.

He felt so good between her legs—so big. Instinctively her bare thighs tightened around him, and the friction of her skin against the tough denim was exquisite. Their tongues met and duelled fiercely, stroking, sucking. Between Sidonie's legs she spasmed and squirmed, seeking more contact with Alexio.

She was barely aware of one of his big hands leaving her face and going to the bottom of her T-shirt, tugging it up, urging her to lift her arms so he could lift it off completely, breaking the contact between their mouths to do so.

She opened her eyes and felt dizzy. Her T-shirt was a blur of grey behind Alexio, hanging precariously on the stool. Now she only wore her panties.

He looked down between their bodies and his hot gaze rested on her bared breasts. Sidonie had been naked in front of a man before…but it had never felt like this. As if she was on fire from the inside out. Her breasts literally throbbed for his touch. Aching…

He cupped them, making her flesh tingle. His thumbs rubbed back and forth across her tight, sensitised nipples and Sidonie dragged in a painful breath. Her heart was beating so loudly she thought it had to be audible.

'You're beautiful…'

Sidonie shook her head, about to deny his compliment, but he took the words out of her mouth as he pushed her back slightly and bent to take one straining peak into his mouth, sucking hard. Sidonie gasped. One hand went to his head, fingers tangling in short silky hair, the other moved behind her, balancing.

It was as if a wire of need was linked directly to the pulse between her legs, tightening the tension inside her, making her arch her back towards him. She felt desperate, wanton. When he moved to her other breast his hand cupped her intimately between her legs, and Sidonie moaned as he pressed against her where every nerve seemed to be screaming out for release.

One of Alexio's fingers slipped behind her underwear

and stroked her where she ached most. Sidonie's breath stopped completely. His mouth was on her breast and that wicked finger was circling, exploring…

She was approaching her peak… She could sense it… The rhythmic pulsations of her body were gathering force—and then Alexio abruptly pulled back and stood up. Sidonie had to put her hands on his hips to stay upright. Everything had turned molten inside her.

'Not here…' he said roughly, his breath uneven.

'Wh—?'

But Sidonie's question was halted as she was scooped up into Alexio's arms and he strode through the apartment to the stairs. Her arms had gone around his neck automatically and the friction of his chest against her deeply sensitised breasts was almost excruciating.

She looked at his face and his jaw was tight. He glanced down at her and that sexy mouth tipped up at one corner. Butterflies danced with the lava in her belly.

He said, 'I refuse to take you on a pool table for the first time. I've been fantasising all day about laying you out and tasting every inch of you, and for that we need a bed.'

The heat inside Sidonie shot to boiling point at the thought of him *fantasising* about this, and at the thought of being spreadeagled, naked, for this man to explore. And that this would be their *first* time, not their only time.

'Oh…' was all she could manage as Alexio shouldered his way into his room, which was dark apart from one low light in the corner and the glittering lights of the city outside.

When he got to the bed he laid Sidonie down and stood back. She was breathless. Her body was still hovering on the edge of fulfilment and she ached for completion. But she sensed that Alexio wasn't about to allow either of them a quick release.

As if reading her mind, he said throatily, 'I want you so

much that I'm tempted to take you now, hard and fast... I want to...'

She'd never experienced hard and fast. She'd experienced mundane and underwhelming. Feeling unaccountably shy, although she was all but naked and panting for the man, Sidonie said in a small voice, 'I don't mind...'

Alexio shook his head and looked grim, his hands going to his jeans, where Sidonie's eyes dropped to watch with mounting fascination.

'No, you don't get off that easily—not after that little sideshow back there.'

Sidonie couldn't drag her gaze back up. She could only watch, helpless, as Alexio opened his buttons and then pushed his jeans down, taking his underwear with them. Her eyes widened and she went even hotter, if that was possible. He was...*magnificent*. And *big*.

A shiver of trepidation ran through her and finally she managed to look at him.

He almost grimaced at her wide eyes. 'Another reason why this won't be hard and fast... I need to make sure you're ready... I don't want to hurt you.'

His concern made Sidonie's chest constrict, and even through the heat haze engulfing her she was aware of a little voice: *danger...danger...*

But then Alexio was bending over her, his big hands making quick work of her underwear, tugging it off her hips and down her legs.

He stood back and looked at her again. Sidonie wanted to turn away and hide herself. Instantly self-conscious. Was he measuring her up against his last lover? Finding her wanting? A disappointment? Did the fact that she wasn't shaved everywhere turn him off?

She brought her arm over her breasts and turned her head, unable to watch him looking at her so intently. And then the bed dipped and his long, powerful body was beside her, legs touching hers, his erection between them, his arms coming around her.

'Don't feel shy…' His hand tipped her chin towards him so she had to meet his gaze. 'You're beautiful…and I want you more than I've ever wanted anyone.'

Sidonie looked into those gorgeous exotic eyes and searched for some hint of insincerity. She couldn't see it. She could see something, though—something unguarded for a moment, as if he was surprised by what he'd said. She was afraid of the tug of emotion in the pit of her being.

Suddenly Sidonie was aware of thinking too much again, and she put her hand up to touch his jaw, reached up to kiss him. All she knew was that she wanted him too—more than anything she'd ever experienced.

When he drew her into his body so that they were touching length to length a wave of intense desire washed through her, brushing aside any doubts and questions. She wanted Alexio to slide into her right then, couldn't bear the thought of the drawn-out torture he'd promised to inflict, and as if reading her mind—*again*—he stopped and pulled back for a moment.

His voice was guttural. 'I don't think I can wait—as much as I want to…'

Sidonie moved so that his leg slid between hers. She could feel how wet she was, ready for him, and she moved against his thigh. His eyes flared.

'I don't want you to wait… I need you too.'

It was a primal, urgent request. Alexio reached behind him to a small cabinet by the bed and took something out. Sidonie realised what it was when he ripped open the foil packet and stroked the condom onto his thick length.

Pressing her down, Alexio came over her, pushing her legs apart. He reached between them and touched her with his fingers, stroking her, entering her. She bent her knees on either side of him and had to bite the inside of her cheek to stop herself from begging him to stop...to go on.

And then he took his hand away and he was guiding the thickness of his erection to her soft folds, pushing in gently, stretching her. Pushing deeper. He was awe-inspiring as he loomed over her. Shoulders broad and powerful, chest sheened with sweat. He pushed her knees further apart, baring her to him completely. Demanding she open up to him.

Something was happening inside Sidonie—some awakening. She'd had sex before, but this felt different. Infinitely different. Slowly, inch by torturous inch, Alexio slid into her, giving her time to adapt and take him, his eyes never leaving hers. She saw sweat break out on his brow, felt the tension in his big body.

'*Moro mou*...you're so tight...'

Instinctively Sidonie tilted her hips, forcing Alexio to thrust deeper, and the movement made her gasp. He filled her now completely.

'Are you okay?' he asked.

Sidonie was speechless. But she nodded. She *was* okay. More than okay. She felt whole, joined to him like this. She moved her hips again experimentally and Alexio drew out a little. Her body clasped at him as he went, already relishing the moment when he would slide back in again, seeking for that delicious friction.

With slow, deliberate thrusts Alexio moved in and out, and the storm grew again inside Sidonie, increasing in its strength and power. With every move of Alexio's body within hers something tightened inside her. He thrust a little harder and Sidonie welcomed it, feeling it burn but not noticing because she ached for it too much.

The tempo changed, became more desperate. Sidonie was aware of small sounds coming from her mouth—moans and laboured breathing, incoherent words. Alexio's body moved faster within hers now, gathering pace. He came closer, hands cupping her face, tangling in her hair, as his mouth met hers and his body thrust powerfully over and over again.

His tongue stabbed deep and she stroked him fiercely, teeth nipping, holding him to her with a desperation as they raced together, hearts thumping in unison.

Sidonie's arms were around his neck, her breasts pressed flat against his chest. She wrapped her legs around his hips. The crescendo was building, leaving her no control over anything. She was part of something huge, magical. Their mouths clung, their kisses became more desperate, biting, and then, just when she thought her body would break in two with the building tension, it broke apart into a million tiny pieces on a wave of orgasmic pleasure, robbing Sidonie of every rational thought. She was flung high into a place she'd never dreamed existed.

Alexio's powerful body thrust one more time and he broke free of their kiss and shouted out as his release swept him up too, seconds behind her.

Sidonie realised she was trembling in the aftermath and was horrified. She tried to pull away from Alexio but he only dragged her closer, wrapping his arms around her until the tremors ceased. She felt more than a little over-whelmed. Alexio pulled his head back and looked at her. She was almost afraid to look at him—afraid he might see something she wasn't ready to expose yet.

'Sidonie...?'

Reluctantly she looked at him and his eyes were molten, still. It had an instant effect on her body. Already. She felt ashamed. How could she want him again so soon?

He was frowning now, pulling away from her, and she tried not to be acutely aware of her nakedness, of feeling vulnerable.

He rested on one elbow. 'Did I hurt you? You weren't innocent?'

Sidonie came up on one elbow too. She shook her head, her hair falling forward. Alexio brushed it back and something about that small gesture heartened her. 'No,' she admitted huskily. 'I've been with a couple of guys. In college. But…it was never like that…I didn't…'

She stopped and went puce, looked down at the sheet. Predictably Alexio tipped her chin up again, not letting her escape.

'You didn't…what? Come like that?'

Sidonie shook her head, mortified to be talking about this when she imagined that his usual post-coital repartee must be far more sophisticated. Still, she was stuck now.

'No,' she got out. 'I mean, I've…*come*…before, but not during sex. Not with a guy.'

Alexio's voice seemed to drop an octave and it sent shivers of sensation right to her core. 'You mean you've experienced it when you've…?'

'Done it to myself. Yes…'

Sidonie glared at him now, beyond embarrassed, and not remotely mollified by the way his eyes had darkened suspiciously. 'Can we stop talking about this now?'

Sidonie reached for the sheet, trying to tuck it around her, but Alexio swatted her hands away and pulled her into him, making her gasp when tender flesh came into contact with his fast reviving arousal.

'I'm glad you told me,' he said gruffly. 'And those guys were idiots.'

The embarrassment drained away, leaving Sidonie feeling the effects of their lovemaking again. Her body was sensitive all over, but sated in a way that was truly wicked.

With awe-inspiring strength Alexio scooped her up and took her into the bathroom with its black-tiled shower. He put her down, keeping an arm around her, and leaned in to turn on the powerful spray. Then he walked her into the shower, following right behind her.

It was pure bliss to have steaming water pounding her skin and then Alexio's big hands, soapy, running all over her body. Over her breasts and belly, down between her legs, across her buttocks. His touch wasn't overtly sexual, but she could see his erection and her body hummed with satisfaction, ready to flare fully back to life if only she wasn't feeling equally ready to crawl into a small space and sleep.

She could only sag against the wall and look at him, so huge and dark in the hot mist, like some kind of pagan warrior. She was boneless, and as if he could sense the lethargy rolling through her body he turned off the spray and wrapped her in a towel, rubbing her brusquely before scooping up her long hair and wrapping it up turban-style.

Then he picked her up again and Sidonie protested weakly. 'I *can* walk, you know.' But even as she said the words she doubted that she could walk right now.

Alexio pulled back the covers and laid her gently on the bed. Sidonie's eyes were already closing and she fought to keep them open, aware of the towel on her head.

'My hair will be frizzy…' she protested sleepily.

Alexio pulled a cover over her, still naked and damp from the shower himself. Sidonie was very aware of that.

'Shh, it'll be fine. You need to rest now. I'll be back in a minute.' He pressed his mouth to her forehead.

Sidonie cracked her eyes open enough to see Alexio drag on his jeans, leaving them tantalisingly open, before he walked out of the room. And then it was too much to fight. She slid into sweet oblivion.

CHAPTER FIVE

WHEN ALEXIO POURED whisky into the glass his hand was shaking. He'd had to get away from Sidonie and he cursed himself for thinking it would be a good idea to take her into the shower. Washing her supple body, seeing her delicate skin marked after their making love and knowing he couldn't touch her again so soon, had been a torture he wouldn't inflict on an enemy.

He'd barely been able to walk away from her in bed, even though her eyes had been closing.

Sex. It had been sex. Alexio knew all about sex. He'd been having it and excelling at it pretty much since he'd been seduced by the sister of a friend of his older brother at the age of fifteen.

But what he'd just experienced up there in his bedroom, with someone he'd met mere hours before, had not been any kind of sex he knew. It had blown his mind. And yet they'd done nothing kinky… Apart from that little striptease downstairs it had been perfectly straightforward. Sidonie obviously wasn't experienced.

Alexio's brain struggled to grapple with this anomaly. Was it that? That she was a little gauche? Was his palate so jaded that the sheer novelty of an inexperienced lover turned him on?

But he knew in his gut it was more than that. Deeper. And he hated to admit it. Alexio threw the whisky down his throat as if it could burn away the hunger that was already building again, which had abated only for mere seconds after his orgasm. He prided himself on his stamina, but this was ridiculous.

When he went back into his room Sidonie had shifted to lie on her front. The sheet clung precariously to her bottom, barely hiding its voluptuous swell, and those dimples were making his mouth water. Her hair had come out of the towel, which had been flung aside haphazardly, and the damp strawberry golden tresses were spread out around her head like glowing halo.

Alexio curled his hands into fists. No way could he go near her on that bed and not rouse her and make love to her again. Silently he turned and took his aching body to his office, where he tried to distract himself with some work.

After staring at the computer screen for a while and seeing nothing but the memory of Sidonie's face as he'd slid into her tight body for the first time, he sat back and rubbed his hands over his face. This was crazy. He was useless. He needed Sidonie again. *Now*.

When he padded back into the bedroom she had moved again and now lay on her back, the sheet pulled up, just about covering her breasts. She moved minutely, as if sensing him. He came close to the bed and saw those dark lashes flutter on pale cheeks scored with pink. Her mouth moved and he wanted to cover it with his. His gaze was riveted to its lush lines and he wondered again how he'd dismissed her at first glance.

'Hey…'

Her husky voice startled him. Her eyes were open, slumberous. Shy. Something punched him in the gut. He had the bizarre feeling that everything in his life up till now had been a bit of a blur and he quashed it ruthlessly. This was no different from anything he'd done before. It was a little more intense, maybe…good chemistry. That was it.

'Hey, yourself…mind if I join you?'

Sidonie shook her head and Alexio undid his jeans, taking them off. When he got into bed he couldn't *not* reach for Sidonie and she came willingly, her arms sliding around him like missing pieces of a jigsaw fitting together. Their mouths found each other and before Alexio could articulate another word he was giving up any attempt to rationalise what was happening because the urge not to think and just to *act* was stronger than anything he could resist.

'I want you to come to Greece with me.'

Sidonie was in paradise. A paradise where she felt at peace and sated and in a state of bliss she'd only ever read about. And that gorgeous voice…

'Sid…wake up.'

Sid. No one had ever called her that before. She liked it. A mouth brushed hers and Sidonie instinctively followed it, seeking more. The by now familiar spurt of desire and awareness was rousing her. *Arousing* her.

She opened her eyes to see Alexio's hard-boned stunning face and bare torso. She was aware of light flooding the big sparse room. Daylight. She blinked. Alexio hovered over her on one arm. His jaw was dark with stubble and she recalled feeling the delicious abrasion on her skin, her thighs. Her belly swooped alarmingly. A jumble of X-rated images tumbled through her mind and she had to breathe to try and not let them overwhelm her.

She remembered him waking her last night…making love to her again. Showing her that the first time, as spectacular as it had been, had only been a precursor. She'd never known it could be like that—so intensely, violently pleasurable. So altering. She felt different.

Alexio was looking at her, waiting for her to say something. Her voice felt rusty, hoarse from crying out over and over again. 'What did you say?'

His hand was on her bare belly under the sheet now and it quivered. Instantly Sidonie's body came to life, nerves tingling, skin tightening. As if well aware of his effect on her, Alexio moved his hand up with exquisite slowness until he cupped her breast, trapping her nipple between his fingers, tightening it gently, enough to pinch.

Sidonie sucked in a breath, wide awake now.

'I said,' he repeated, 'I want you to come to Greece with me. I have a place on Santorini. I've decided to take a few days' break…'

Sidonie automatically went to shake her head but Alexio's hand left her breast and swept up to cup her chin.

Softly he said, 'We've been here before, Sid…you know what happens if you say no to me.'

Sid. The way he said it made her feel as if she were drowning—as if she'd known this man for aeons when it had been a mere twenty-four hours. All she could see were those amazing golden-green eyes, hypnotising her. Drugging her.

'You said yourself you don't have a job to go back to…so why not extend your trip for a few days? Come with me… and I'll show you paradise.'

He bent his head to kiss Sidonie and she felt like letting out a short, shocked laugh. He'd already unwittingly shown her paradise. But then his mouth was on hers and she couldn't think. She struggled to try and focus. She knew that her aunt was safe and secure for a couple of weeks. All that responsibility hovered in the wings, but it didn't have to be dealt with right at this moment—could she stretch one night into a few days? She wanted to, with a fierceness that surprised her.

As Alexio moved over her body, sinking his hips between her thighs, his erection hard and ready, Sidonie was melting, weakening. She wasn't ready to walk away yet…

she wanted more of this man. More of this fantasy. More
of this wicked self-indulgence.

She wrapped her arms around his neck and opened her
legs to him and then, when he stopped kissing her for a few
seconds, just before he joined their bodies, Sidonie looked
up at him and said huskily, 'Okay...I'll come with you.'

Alexio Christakos was a magician. A sexy, devilish magician. Just over twenty-four hours after meeting him he had
magicked her to an island in another country. Where everything was painted blue and white, where the sun sparkled
overhead, and where the glittering sea stretched as far as
the eye could see. There was nothing but the hazy shapes
of more islands in the distance to break the horizon line.

Her hand was wrapped tightly in his as he showed her
around his stupendously gorgeous villa near Oia, on the
north-west coast of Santorini. Sidonie could feel the faint
burn of secret muscles after the long hours of intense lovemaking the previous night. If she stopped to think about it
all for a second she might explode...so she bit her lip and
tried not to gape as he showed her into the master suite,
which led directly out to a terrace featuring an infinity pool.

He glanced back at her, saying, 'I know you didn't exactly come prepared...there are some clothes here for your
use.'

Sidonie watched as he let her hand go to open double
doors which led into a walk-in closet. His clothes were
hung up and laid out on the left hand side and the right
hand side was bursting with a glorious kaleidoscope of
colours and textures.

A funny pain lanced her chest. Of *course* he had a wardrobe stocked with women's clothes. This had to be a fre-
quent pitstop for him with his lovers/mistresses. He was a
generous man. She was sure many of the garments must
still be unworn.

To buy time, and hide her reaction, Sidonie reached out and fingered a piece of silk which felt as delicate as air in her hands.

This whole experience was transitory and all this was doing was driving the point home. She had to *not* think about things like how attentive he'd been on the flight to Athens on his private jet—distracting her from her fear of flying with drugging kisses. Or the revelation on the helicopter flight to the island that instead of feeling her fear increasing she'd felt exhilarated.

Sidonie forced herself to smile and said with bright joviality, 'Well, at least I won't have to worry about washing my knickers out in the sink. I'm sure your housekeeper would be horrified.'

She looked at him and her smile slipped a little as she saw something hard in his eyes—something she hadn't seen before. But before she could dwell on it he'd stabbed his fingers deep in her hair and tipped her face up to his, distracting her with a mind-altering kiss.

When he finally pulled away they were breathing harshly and Sidonie's body trembled all over. She still wasn't used to this unprecedented physical reaction—as if she were some kind of a puppet and he could control her responses at will. It made her feel intensely vulnerable.

'Get changed and let's go for a swim.'

Sidonie burned at the thought of seeing Alexio's seminaked body just for her private pleasure.

She managed a rough-sounding, 'Okay.'

And when he gently turned her around and pushed her in the direction of that wall of clothes again Sidonie tried in vain to stem the flood of emotions that made her hands shake as she searched for the relevant garments.

Sidonie wrapped her legs around Alexio's waist and her arms around his neck. His back was broad, strong and smooth between her legs and against her chest. They were both wet and salty after swimming in the sea at the bottom of a precipitious set of stone steps leading directly down from the villa. His arms were looped under her thighs as he carried her piggyback-style back up.

The sun was hot on Sidonie's back and Alexio grumbled good-naturedly, 'I'm not a mule, you know.'

She grinned and pressed a kiss to Alexio's neck, feeling his arms tighten under her legs. 'I know. You're much, much better-looking than a mule, and far more comfortable.'

She rested her head on his shoulder for a moment, squinting her eyes at the glittering endless azure blue of the sea. Three days had passed since they'd arrived at his villa. Three days of sun, sea and... She blushed at the thought of all the mind-blowing sex.

They'd only left the villa once. Yesterday evening Alexio had taken her out on a small boat into the Caldera where he'd surprised her with a light supper complete with wine. They'd had prime position for watching the famous Santorini sunset and Sidonie had never seen anything so stunning or special.

She'd felt absurdly emotional at the beauty of everything...at the experience that this man was unwittingly giving her when her life was about to change so dramatically. She was storing up every moment—morsels she would take out at a later date and comfort herself with.

An all but invisible housekeeper at the villa left out food at strategic times, so she and Alexio had done little but eat and sleep and make love. Sidonie felt sated on a level she'd never known before. Sated...but curiously unfulfilled too.

Conversation with Alexio never went beyond the superficial. It felt almost as if the level of closeness and intimacy she'd experienced when they'd first met had been closed off.

But then what had she expected? This was transient.

Alexio didn't do relationships, and neither was she in any position to cleave herself to a man.

Sidonie had realised that the only way she could get through this and remain in any way protected was to try and fool Alexio into believing that this wasn't half as special for her as it really was. So she was doing her best to project an air of vague nonchalance. Every time her mouth wanted to drop open in awe, or she wanted to squeal with excitement, she reined it in.

Because if she let her guard slip for a second Sidonie was terrified he would read the depth of her emotions— and as she wasn't even prepared to inspect them herself she certainly wasn't ready for his laser-like gaze to see them.

'I want to take you out tonight.'

Sidonie murmured something indistinct. Her cheek rested on Alexio's chest and one of her legs was thrown over his thighs. He could feel his body stir against her and despite the sated languor of his body he could have groaned. When would it end? This ever-present hunger?

His fingers trailed up and down Sidonie's spine. After carrying her up the steps from the sea earlier he'd walked her straight underneath the outdoor shower on his terrace, near the glittering infinity pool. The cool spray had done little to stem hisdesire. Within seconds Sidonie had been in his arms, her body pressed against his, and they'd inevitably ended up in bed.

Alexio forced his mind from the memory because it made him uncomfortable. 'Did you hear me, Sid? I want to take you out tonight...'

Sidonie eventually lifted her head and looked at Alexio with slumberous eyes and deliciously tousled hair. 'You might have to give me a piggyback again.'

Alexio tipped her chin up, averting her hungry gaze

from his mouth to his eyes. 'No. You're not going to tempt me again. We'll pretend we're civilised if it kills us.'

Sidonie shifted slightly so that she was moving on top of Alexio. His blood started to sizzle all over again. She spread her thighs either side of him and her breasts touched his chest, the hard nipples scraping against his chest hair, making him thicken with need.

He could see something in her eyes—something innately feminine and full of wicked mystery. She wriggled her bottom so that his erection pressed against her body, where she was already damp, ready for him again. And just like that Alexio had to give up any pretence that he could be civilised.

He took her hips in his hands, pushing her back so that he could thrust up and into her. Sidonie gasped at the intrusion and then sighed voluptuously as her body began to move against him, the delicious dance of desire starting all over again.

'Witch...' Alexio muttered as their movements became more urgent and they gave themselves up to the inexorable ride into ecstasy.

Alexio was waiting for Sidonie to emerge from the villa after her shower late that evening. The sun had set a while ago. They'd watched it from a lounger by the pool, both languid after their intense lovemaking. The spectacular sky was now fading into a faint orange and pink hue and the famous lights of Santorini's west coast were coming on.

Alexio was oblivious to it, though. He was feeling more and more off-balance. Exposed. And, even worse, vulnerable. The last time he'd felt like this had been in front of his mother as a child, when she'd coldly infected him with her cynicism. From then till now it had formed a part of his protective armour. It had become a second skin, and everything in his life had merely compounded his world view.

As soon as he'd turned his back on his inheritance so publicly his coterie of so-called friends and hangers-on had left him—apart from one or two people and his brother. Then, as soon as he'd shown signs of making a fortune, they'd come back in their droves.

Nothing much had surprised him after that telling experiment in human nature—as if he hadn't had enough lessons from his parents. *Until Sidonie.* She surprised him. She was like a whirling dervish, smashing everything in her path and taking him with her. He'd had no intention of taking a few days' holiday until he'd woken up beside her in London the morning after that night and felt the insistent throb of hunger in his blood and his body.

No way could he have let her go.

He'd known one night wouldn't be enough, but he'd felt then as if a month wouldn't be long enough to sate himself with her. Feeling slightly panicked, Alexio had decided that the best thing to do would be to take her away, so that he could indulge this desire day and night and let it burn out.

However, this was the third night, and he felt as if a lifetime wouldn't be enough to sate himself with Sidonie. He'd done his best to hold her at a distance, deliberately curbing the way she made him want to relax and speak whatever was on his mind. But it was hard. And getting harder.

When she'd leapt onto his back earlier, to be carried up the steps, Alexio's chest had swelled with an emotion that had made him shake. No woman he knew was so impulsive, so tactile, so effortlessly affectionate.

Yet despite her easy affection she wasn't suffocating him with emotion—far from it. She was holding back—exuding an air of nonchalance.

Something dark inside him had raised its ugly head. *Suspicion.* He remembered showing her the closet full of clothes on that first day. He'd expected shock, awe, gushing gratitude. Even his most cynical lovers never failed to put on an act when he presented them with gifts. But Sidonie, whom he would never have put in their category, had been completely blasé, and since then he hadn't been able to push down a niggle of disquiet.

One minute she was like an open book, her expressions as unguarded as a child's and equally disarming. The next she was as mysterious as the Sphinx, exhibiting an age-old feminine mystique that made him wonder if he was being completely naïve.

Alexio didn't like the reminder that from the moment he'd met Sidonie on that plane he'd been acting out of character. He *never* encouraged a woman to stay overnight in his apartment, even if they'd had dinner there. And he certainly never took off at a moment's notice, throwing his normally rigid schedule out of the window.

The growing doubt had prompted Alexio to put in a call to his most trusted employee and personal friend—his solicitor—just a short while before. He was one of the few who had stuck by Alexio's side through his lean times. Pushing down a feeling of guilt, he had instructed him to engage someone to do a background check into Sidonie.

His friend had chuckled. 'I thought you only did this when you wanted to take over another company or find an adversary's weak points? Now you're including your lovers?'

He'd answered far more curtly than he'd intended. 'Just do it, Demetrius. I don't expect a discussion about it.'

Despite the guilt he'd felt at taking such action, when Alexio had put the phone down he'd felt some semblance of equilibrium return. Sidonie hadn't scrambled his head so badly that he wasn't still aware of protecting himself. He *was* in control.

That control was about to be shot to pieces, though, as he heard a sound and turned around. Sidonie had emerged onto the terrace and for a long second Alexio literally lost his breath. All he could feel was his heart pounding as it struggled without oxygen.

The dress was a burnt orange colour and silk. Looped over one shoulder, and strapless on the other side, It had a big hole cut out over one hip, showing off the naked indentation of Sidonie's waist. A hint of one breast was visible just above the top of the dress as it swooped over her chest, hugging the delicious curve. The silk fell to her knees, but one leg peeped out of a thigh-high slit.

She was wearing nothing that he hadn't already seen on other lovers. He'd seen far less. But Alexio had to battle the very strong urge to tell her to go back and change, like an over-protective father. Or a mindlessly jealous lover, imagining the effect she'd have on other men. That thought alone made him stop and take in a breath. His chest swelled painfully.

'Is it okay?'

Sidonie was frowning, plucking at the dress. She looked at Alexio and this was one of those moments when she looked endearingly exposed, reminding him of the woman he'd met on the plane—all at once spiky and yet vulnerable.

'Come here,' he husked.

Sidonie moved towards him and Alexio had to bite back a groan of need. One long, slender leg was displayed in all its provocative glory as she walked towards him, her dainty feet encased in gold peeptoe heels.

She stopped before him and looked up. Her hair lay loose and long around her shoulders, glinting like golden fire in the dusky light. Her skin had already taken on a golden glow from the sun, despite the copious amounts of factor fifty he'd insisted she keep putting on—much to her disgust. Her freckles had exploded and magnified across her nose and cheeks. And her shoulders.

When Alexio finally felt able to touch her without tipping her over his shoulder and taking her back inside, he slid a hand around the back of her neck. That silky fall of hair against his hand made his body throb.

'You look…stunning.'

The vulnerability he'd seen dissipated and Sidonie smiled. 'Thank you…so do you.'

Alexio was used to compliments and they always felt empty. Except when she said it. He took his hand away, because he knew if he did something like kiss her now he'd never stop. Instead he took her hand and led her out of the villa to a nearby hidden garage which housed a sports car—one of his brother's new models.

It was a convertible, and Sidonie whistled in appreciation as she got in. Alexio held the door open for her, trying his best not to look at her exposed leg. Dammit, maybe he *should* get her to change?

Gritting his jaw, and wondering why on earth he'd thought taking her out would be a good idea, he got in the other side and soon they were driving along the coast, towards the bustling night-life of Fira.

As Alexio's car swept them along the coast of the island, and the sky became darker over the expanse of the sea, the lights of the houses and dwellings and the approaching town of Fira made everything look like a fairytale. Alexio was driving relatively slowly on the narrow roads and the cool evening air was delicious on Sidonie's sun-heated skin.

She shivered when she thought about how gorgeous Alexio had looked on the terrace against the setting sun, dressed in a dark suit with a dark shirt. The more time she spent with him, the more gorgeous he seemed to get. She felt weak inside when she thought of how protective he was, too, making sure she wore a high-factor cream in the sun.

'But I want to get *some* colour!' Sidonie had protested earlier.

Alexio had held her down easily on the lounger and proceeded to slather her with cream, saying sternly, 'You are *not* damaging your skin.'

Then she'd got so distracted by where his hands were going that she hadn't had the strength to fight him...

'Are you cold?'

Sidonie blushed in the darkening light and shook her head. 'No, I'm fine. I like the freshness.'

Alexio looked back to the road. 'I should have made you bring a jacket. It still gets cool at night this time of year.'

Sidonie smiled. 'You can't help yourself, can you?'

'Can't help what?'

'Being protective. I bet you were like that with your mother.'

Alexio made a noise then. It sounded like something between a snort and a cough and Sidonie looked at him. After a minute he glanced at her and she could see that his jaw was tense. The air was definitely cooler now.

'Believe me...' his tone was icy '...my mother did not need a protector. Anything but.'

Sidonie frowned, 'Why do you say that? What was she like?'

Alexio's jaw got even tighter. Sidonie could see it reflected in the lights of the dashboard.

'She was self-contained. Aloof. And she didn't need anyone.'

Sidonie held in a gasp at his stark words. 'Everyone needs someone—even if they don't want to admit it. You make her sound lonely.'

Eventually Alexio responded, just as the town of Fira came into view. 'Maybe she was... But I don't really want to discuss my mother when we have far more exciting things to talk about—like where I'm going to take you clubbing.'

Sidonie felt the door slam in her face with his terse delivery. His personal life was obviously a no-go area. She thought of the darkness in her own past, and how she'd hate for Alexio to know about it, and figured maybe it was for the best that he wasn't inviting this kind of intimacy.

She turned and faced the front and saw the stunning cavalcade of lights in the town as it seemed to drop precipitously to the gaping black of the sea. Momentarily distracted, Sidonie breathed, 'This is beautiful.'

Alexio was parking the car outside an upmarket-looking hotel and a young man was rushing out. 'We have to walk from here; the streets are pedestrianised,' Alexio explained as he got out.

He threw the keys to the young man, who was all but drooling at the sight of the stunning car, then came around to Sidonie's door and opened it for her, giving her his hand to help her out. Sidonie felt shaky and insecure at the thought of being seen in public with Alexio.

He kept her hand in his and said a few words in Greek to the man, whose face went pale. Then they walked away.

'What did you say to him?' Sidonie asked curiously.

Alexio smiled. 'I told him that if I came back to find one mark on the car I'd break his legs.'

'Oh…' Sidonie held in a giggle when she thought of the man paling so dramatically. 'Well, that makes things clear for him.' Her fingers tightened around his hand and she looked up. 'You wouldn't, though, would you? Break his legs?'

Alexio stopped and looked down, horrified, 'Of course not—what do you take me for? I just told him he'd be paying me out of his wages for the rest of his life.'

Sidonie tucked her other arm around Alexio's and said with mock relief, 'Okay—that's so much better than broken legs.'

Alexio looked down. He could see the smile playing around Sidonie's mouth, and that tantalising glimpse of long and slender leg. He could feel her breast against his arm and had to grit his jaw. It still felt tight after her questions about his mother… *'You make her sound lonely.'*

The truth was that Alexio had always had the impression that his mother *had* been lonely, and he didn't like the way Sidonie's innocent comments had brought him back to a time when it had been all too apparent that he couldn't protect his mother simply because she would not allow it. Not even when she needed it.

He forced his train of thought away from that unwelcome memory. They were approaching a narrow street with a glittering array of jewellery shops and Sidonie had stopped, enthralled, outside the first one.

She sighed deeply and sent a quick rueful glance to Alexio. 'I have to admit to a deeply unattractive trait: a love for glittery objects. My father used to say I was like a magpie, obsessed with shiny things. I used to collect the most random objects and put them in a box in my room and then take them out to look at them.'

Sidonie looked at the display again and Alexio couldn't stop the prickle of something across the back of his neck. The sensation of exposure was strong, along with something like disappointment. A feeling of inevitability. This was what he was used to. Women cajoling, seeking something. And even though Sidonie wasn't going about it in a way he was used to wasn't it the same thing? She was hinting that she loved jewellery and that she expected him to spoil her with some.

She looked up at him then and must have seen something in his expression. She frowned. 'What is it?'

Quickly he schooled his features. 'Nothing.' His voice was tight. 'The club is just down here.'

CHAPTER SIX

SIDONIE FELT AS if she'd done something wrong. The look on Alexio's face just now had been almost...*disgusted*. She felt stupid for blurting out that she'd always loved glittery things. It was a trait that she'd inherited from her mother and Sidonie didn't like to be reminded of that. Especially when she knew deep down that it wasn't like her mother's love for real jewels. When she'd found her childhood jewellery box during the clearing of the house after her father had died she could almost have laughed, because it was full of ten-cent pieces, buttons and tin foil. Hardly a treasure trove.

Sidonie tried to push down the sense of disquiet and followed Alexio into a very mysterious-looking doorway with no name on it. A man in a black suit with an earpiece let them in with a deferential nod to Alexio.

Determined to put his reaction out of her mind, Sidonie tightened her hand reflexively in Alexio's and he looked down at her. She was relieved to see that the tightness in his expression was gone and that the lazy, sexy insouciance was back.

Another entrance was just ahead, with billowing white curtains wafting in the breeze. A stunning glamazon of a woman stepped out, dressed in a tiny black dress which showcased her astounding body.

Sidonie nearly tripped over her heels and Alexio steadied her, looking down. 'Okay?'

Sidonie nodded, still struck dumb by the dark-haired Greek beauty who was now greeting Alexio *very warmly* with kisses on each cheek—far too close to his mouth for Sidonie's liking. She felt something rise within her—something hot and acrid. *Jealousy.*

The woman turned her gaze on Sidonie and dismissed her with a cool glance before turning back to Alexio. She pouted ruby-red lips and proceeded to talk to Alexio in Greek, which Sidonie of course couldn't follow.

Alexio replied in English, though, saying, 'I've been too busy to come back. This is Sidonie—Sidonie, this is Elettra.'

Sidonie smiled, but the other women barely smiled back at all. It was like the air hostess all over again. Far from making Sidonie feel triumphant that she had the man everyone wanted, it only made her feel insecure. Was Alexio even now looking at this woman and wishing he was availing himself of her charms instead of gauche, inexperienced Sidonie's?

But then the sight of the interior of the club took every thought out of Sidonie's head. It was a massive, cavernous, breathtaking space. Dark and dimly lit with what seemed to be a thousand lanterns. A huge bar took up one entire wall. There was a dance floor with glowing boxes of neon lights in the old Studio 54 style. There were booths and private tables dotted around the place, and then there was a whole other level down below which was already heaving with people.

Beautiful people were everywhere. Funky music throbbed from the sound system. It was achingly hip and exclusive.

Elettra was leading them to a booth, her hips swaying sinuously in her teeny-tiny dress. When they got there Sidonie could see that they had a bird's eye view of the entire place, and almost immediately after Elettra left—with clear reluctance—an equally stunning-looking waitress was there to take their orders. She was dressed in tiny shorts and a white shirt with very low-cut buttons. She had a pinafore-style apron that did little to detract from the sexiness of the outfit—if anything it fetishised it slightly.

Sidonie felt seriously out of her depth.

After Alexio had given an order he leant back and looked at her. She knew she must look like some wide-eyed hick.

'Well? What do you think?'

Sidonie sat back, overwhelmed, and gave a little laugh. 'I think that we're not in Kansas any more, Toto.'

Alexio frowned and Sidonie explained with a wave of her hand. 'When Dorothy ends up in Oz…' She shook her head. 'This is out of this world. I've never seen anything like it. I'm used to grimy college student bars.'

The waitress came back with small plates of finger food and a bottle of champagne. Sidonie groaned softly. She hadn't realised she was hungry and she stole a glance at Alexio, who was watching her with amusement.

'My appetite is just one big joke to you, isn't it?'

He shrugged and prepared some pitta bread and tzatziki, handing it to her. She ate it with relish and took a sip of the sparkling wine.

Joking, she said, 'I could get used to this, you know.'

She missed Alexio's enigmatic look as she plucked an olive from a bowl. When she did look at him he was lounging back, regarding her with an expression that had her blood heating up. It was *that* look. The one that made him look hungry and made her feel hungry. But not for food.

'I want to dance with you.'

Sidonie swallowed what she was eating. The mere thought of dancing with this man made any appetite she did have flee. A slow, sexy hip-hop song was playing, its beat sending tremors of sexual awareness through Sidonie's body.

'Okay…'

Moving out of the booth seat, Alexio stood and held out his hand. He looked so young in that moment, and so breathtakingly gorgeous, that Sidonie had to relegate it like a snapshot to the back of her mind because it was too much to deal with.

His hand in hers, Alexio led her to the dance floor, which was filling up with similarly minded couples. He drew her into his arms, close to his body, and it was the most natural thing to loop her hands and arms around his neck.

His hands were possessive on her, sexual. One hand rested over her buttocks. The other slid under the gaping hole at the side of her dress to splay across her naked back. *Lord.* How was she expected to stay standing when he touched her like that? As Sidonie looked into his eyes the infectious beat of the music throbbed through every vein and made her tingle. She realised, not for the first time, how far under her skin he'd sneaked.

There was something so…so up-front and unashamed about him. He was too confident to play games. Too assured. She knew exactly where she stood. And even though that brought misgivings about how cool she was with that— which was a lot less cool than she pretended—she couldn't blame him for her growing confusing emotions. Her attachment.

The fact that she trusted him was huge. She'd never trusted anyone, really…not since those awful days when her mother had exposed a very ugly side of reality and herself. Sidonie suspected now that her highly developed reticence had influenced her experiences with her first two brief relationships. No wonder they'd been unsatisfactory; she hadn't let either of them get too close.

But Alexio… Alexio had smashed through a wall she'd been barely aware of building around herself and now all that remained was rubble. And her exposed beating heart.

It hit her then, as she looked up into those golden compelling eyes…she was falling for him. And it was too late to stop herself.

Her arms tightened around Alexio's neck in automatic rejection of her thought, as if she could ward it off if she squashed it right away. But Alexio couldn't read the stricken nature of her revelation. He saw only those wide aquamarine eyes and felt Sidonie's arms tighten around him and he pulled her even closer.

Her breasts pressed against him, her hips welded to his, and his arousal was urgent and insistent. Damn her. He *never* lost it like this.

Wanting to punish her for something he wasn't even sure of, Alexio cupped the back of her head and, as the throbbing beat of the music changed and got faster, bent his head and took her mouth in a bruising passionate kiss.

As if something was holding her back, Sidonie didn't respond for a moment. Incensed by this, Alexio used every skill in his arsenal to make her respond—and when she did his blood ignited.

After long, drugging moments, Alexio struggled to drag himself away from Sidonie's mouth. He felt dazed. The music was faster now. People were dancing around him. They were the only ones standing still. She was slow to open her eyes. They looked slumberous, filled with hidden depths. Filled with…emotion. Instantly Alexio waited for that cold feeling to infect him, but it didn't.

Before he could feel any more disjointed he all but dragged Sidonie off the dance floor and back to the booth. The food had been cleared away. They sat down and Alexio took a swig of champagne. But it was no good. He couldn't feel civilised sitting next to Sidonie with that provocative dress testing his control every time she moved.

He took her hand and she looked at him. Her mouth was swollen. Her eyes were huge, pupils dilated.

'Let's get out of here…'

She opened her mouth, paling slightly, as if she saw something in his expression that frightened her slightly. He felt feral.

'But we only just got here.'

Alexio forced himself to calm down and tried not to think about the fact that when he usually came to a club with a woman it was a very different experience. He was usually a lot more in control.

Tightly he said, 'If you don't want to go we can stay…'

'Why do you want to go?' she asked, surprising him. Most women would have pouted or sidled up to him, trying to distract him, cajole him.

'Because,' he offered with brutal honesty, 'I'm afraid if we don't leave that I'll get arrested for making love to you in front of an audience, and the last time I checked this wasn't a sex club.'

'Oh…' Sidonie said, in a small voice barely audible above the music. She took a swift sip of her drink and then looked at him. She was all at once shy and confident—again that intriguing mix. 'In that case maybe we should go…'

Relief and anticipation swept through Alexio as he grabbed for her hand and led her out of the booth—this time back to the VIP exit.

The return journey to Alexio's villa in the car was torturous. Sidonie was acutely aware of the thick sexual tension that enveloped them. Alexio had looked so…*primal* back at the club. She hadn't had a chance of pretending everything was normal after that dance and after his bald declaration. She'd wanted them to be alone as badly as he had.

Alexio looked at her now and lifted his arm for her to come close to his side. Sidonie didn't hesitate. She slid her arms around his hard-muscled torso and rested her head on his chest. Alexio's hand found the hole in the side of her dress and sneaked underneath, climbing up until he could cup her breast, his fingers pinching a nipple.

Sidonie's breath grew choppy. Between her legs she was embarrassingly wet.

By the time they reached the garage and he stopped the car Sidonie had to peel herself off Alexio.

He growled softly, 'Where do you think you're going?'

Sidonie stopped and looked at him. He had that look again, and it sent tremors of excitement into her blood. 'Inside?' she said hopefully, already imagining the huge bed.

Alexio shook his head and as he did so moved his seat back. 'No time. I can't wait. Take off your knickers.'

Sidonie's eyes went very big when she saw Alexio's hands go to his belt. He started undoing it. They were going to do it here. Right now. Heat washed up through Sidonie and her hands shook with need as she did as she was bid, sliding her panties off and down her legs.

When they hit the floor of the car Alexio reached for her and brought her over to straddle his lap. Sidonie's heart was out of control as Alexio dragged her dress down to bare one creamy white breast, its nipple already hard and pouting flagrantly for his mouth and tongue.

She groaned out loud when he surrounded it in sucking heat and clasped his head. Her hips were already grinding gently against his lap and the hard bulge she could feel there, still constrained by his trousers. Feeling frustration build, Sidonie reached down, lifting up slightly, and almost wept with relief when she could feel Alexio's naked arousal pushing against her where she ached.

When he thrust up and into her their mingled breaths were harsh in the quiet of the small space. Sidonie could feel the steering wheel digging into her back, the gearshift against her knee, but she didn't care. Her body rose and fell against Alexio's. They were both so turned on and ready that their mutual completion shattered around them in minutes. Sidonie could only sag against him afterwards, her mind a blissful blank of nothingness.

As dawn broke over the eastern side of the island and bathed the western edges in a pink glow Sidonie lay awake, with her cheek resting on Alexio's chest. Despite their frantic coupling in the car as soon as they'd got back, their hunger for one another hadn't been dented.

She knew he was awake too because she could feel the tension in his body. The master bedroom of the villa, despite its vast airiness, felt like a cocoon around them. Sidonie never wanted to leave this place, or this man. For a second she resented the inevitable intrusion of reality and *responsibility*—and then felt immediately guilty when she thought of Tante Josephine. Of course she couldn't expect her aunt to deal with the debts incurred by her mother.

Sighing deeply, Sidonie snuggled closer to Alexio, hating how a shiver went down her spine, as if someone had just walked over her grave.

'What's wrong?'

Sidonie shook her head against him and whispered, 'Nothing.' *Everything*, she didn't say.

A question she'd wanted to ask him for days rose up within her and, longing for a diversion from her own thoughts, she lifted her head and rested her chin on her hand against his chest.

He looked at her and she almost smiled at the wariness of him. As if she were some kind of unexploded device.

'Can I ask you something?'

A small smile played around that gorgeous sexy mouth. 'Do I have a choice?'

'Not really,' Sidonie said cheerfully, and then, 'Why did you turn your back on your inheritance to make your own way?'

She'd asked him the question that first evening in his

apartment but he'd deflected it easily. Now his face became inscrutable, and Sidonie prepared herself for another brush-off, but to her surprise his chest rose and fell in a deep sigh. As if he was giving in.

He said carefully, 'You *do* know that if I tell you I'll have to kill you?'

Sidonie nodded with mock seriousness. 'I know. However, I feel like I've packed a lot into my twenty-three years, so I'm prepared to go if I have to.'

Alexio took some of her hair between his fingers and caressed it, saying, 'Such a pity…but if you're positive…?'

Mock resolute, Sidonie said, 'I'm positive.'

Joking aside, Alexio lifted one shoulder and said, 'It's really not that exciting.'

'I'm intrigued. It's not many people who would turn their back on an Onassis-sized inheritance.'

Alexio grimaced. 'The size of the inheritance was vastly exaggerated…'

Sidonie stayed quiet.

With clear reluctance Alexio told her, 'I am my father's only son. Even though my half-brother grew up with us, my father used to taunt him every day that he would not receive a cent from him. I always resented my father's lack of generosity and the way he wielded his power over everyone else. But I saw how it forged in my brother a will to succeed and prosper on his own. I envied him because he wasn't constrained like I was. Bound to my father's expectations. My father used to pit us against each other all the time, me and my brother.'

Alexio grimaced.

'Obviously this didn't do our relationship much good, and by the time my brother left home it's safe to say we hated each other's guts. My father just assumed I would be joining him in his empire. He never listened to me long enough to know that I had no interest in his shipping business. I rebelled against that expectation. The business wasn't even his—not rightfully. He was the second son and his brother had died at a young age, leaving him in line to take over. His own father hadn't wanted it for him, but my father grabbed it with both hands and ousted my grandfather as soon as he could.'

Sidonie's eyes grew wide. 'But that's so…'

'Ruthless?' Alexio interjected with a grim smile.

Sidonie nodded.

'That's my father's way. To grab at things. Take them. He wanted me to inherit and join him—but not as an equal, as someone he could control.' He sighed. 'In the meantime I saw Rafaele, my brother, single-handedly resurrecting his own family name and business out of the ashes. All those years of rivalry were still in my blood—if he could do it so could I.'

Sidonie spoke softly. 'So when your father expected you to follow in his footsteps you said no?'

Alexio looked into Sidonie's clear eyes and felt in that moment as if he could just spill all the secrets in his guts and keep spilling. It was dangerous. Too dangerous. He stifled the impulse with effort.

'I said no. And walked away. He disinherited me and now here I am.'

'Probably more successful than he is…'

Alexio was surprised that she'd surmised that but it was true. What he didn't tell her, though, was how his success hadn't given him any measure of satisfaction where his father was concerned. It had never been about besting his father. It had been about distancing himself from a man who had made him fear *he* had the same lack of emotional control in his own make-up. Fear that he might be similarly greedy and never experience the thrill of making it on his own as his brother had. Fear that he'd never get away from that sterile house full of tension and hatred. *Violence*.

He felt cold inside all of a sudden.

Just then Alexio's mobile phone beeped on the nearby bedside cabinet. He reached for it and saw the text message icon winking. He opened it and saw it was from his solicitor.

I have information about your Miss Fitzgerald. Call when you get a chance. D.

Instantly something cold slithered into Alexio's gut.

'What is it?' Sidonie asked with obvious concern.

Alexio put the phone back, face down, and looked at her. 'Nothing important.'

Guilt warred with something much deeper inside him. Superstitiously he wanted to pretend he hadn't just seen that text and that there wasn't something dark lurking in the wings.

He came up and hovered over her, feeling that familiar heady rush of desire when he looked at her body, breasts bared and tempting. Her mouth was enticing him ever downwards, where he wouldn't have to think about anything...for a little longer.

'What did you just say?' Alexio asked faintly.

He was stunned. The sun was high outside his villa's office. His body was still humming in the aftermath of seriously pleasurable lovemaking and he couldn't really compute this information.

His solicitor repeated himself. 'Her mother went to jail for two years.'

Alexio went cold all over. 'Jail? Why?'

Demetrius sighed. 'I really wish I didn't have to tell you this. Her mother was prosecuted for stalking and blackmailing her married lover. She'd been doing it for years, in ever increasing amounts. It would appear that her husband, Miss

Fitzgerald's father, wasn't making enough to keep her in the style to which she wanted to be accustomed. Even though it also appears he did his best to try and keep both his wife and daughter in comfort and relative luxury.'

Alexio struggled against the shock. This information was not pleasant, but it hardly condemned Sidonie.

His friend continued, 'When her mother was released they moved to another part of the country to avoid the scandal and Miss Fitzgerald's father's business started to boom. Sidonie went to one of the best local schools, had a pony…the works. Her mother was a regular on the social scene…designer clothes and jewellery. They managed to keep her past a secret for the most part. When the property market collapsed so did her father's business and they lost everything.'

Alexio was feeling increasingly uncomfortable. 'Demetrius, is that it? I think I've heard enough.'

'Well, not quite. I think you should hear the rest. After Mr Fitzgerald died his wife went back to Paris to move in with her younger sister.'

'Demetrius—'

The man butted in. 'Alexio, I did some more digging via some colleagues in Paris and you need to hear this… Sidonie's mother persuaded her sister to take out a mortgage on a flat her husband had bought and paid for years before. She also maxed out credit cards in her sister's name. She died leaving the woman in so much debt that she'll never recover.'

Alexio felt angry now and gritted out, 'What does this have to do with Sidonie?'

'You met her when she was on her way home from Paris?'

'Yes,' Alexio agreed curtly, regretting having ever involved his friend like this.

'She'd just signed an agreement to accept responsibility for all those debts on her aunt's behalf. Now, let me ask you this—has she given any hint at all that she's a woman with a huge financial burden on her shoulders? If not,' his friend went on heavily, 'you have to ask yourself why she's acting as if nothing is wrong.'

When Sidonie woke again she was alone in the bed and for some reason her belly went into a ball of tension. Something was wrong. She could feel it.

She lifted her head and looked around. No sign of Alexio. Maybe he'd gone for a swim? He was a powerful swimmer and liked the sea as opposed to the pool.

Muscles protesting pleasurably as she sat up, Sidonie got out of bed and went to the bathroom, tying her hair up so that it wouldn't get wet in the shower.

When she came out again she rubbed her body dry with a towel and looked at the vast array of clothes hanging in the walk-in wardrobe. Something bitter struck her again to think of his other women, but Sidonie shoved it down. She didn't have the right to feel jealous, possessive.

She found some shorts and a green halterneck top and stuck them on and then went to find Alexio, still with that odd feeling of foreboding in her belly. Before she could leave the bedroom, though, she heard the sound of her phone ringing. She kept it on mainly in case Tante Josephine was looking for her, and when she located it at the bottom of her bag she saw that it *was* her aunt.

Expecting nothing more than her aunt wanting to chat, Sidonie sat on the edge of the bed and answered warmly in French. Her smile faded in an instant, though, when all she could hear were racking sobs from the other end of the phone.

Instantly Sidonie stood up. 'Tante Josephine, what is it? Please try to stop crying...'

Eventually her aunt was able to calm down enough to

start talking, after Sidonie had encouraged her to breathe slowly. Her aunt was prone to panic attacks and Sidonie didn't want one to happen before she could find out what was wrong.

Through fits and starts it transpired that someone on her *vacances* had heard about Tante Josephine's financial woes and put the fear of God into her by telling her all sorts of horror stories about repossessions and jail sentences for not paying debts. No wonder her aunt was hysterical.

But no matter what Sidonie said it didn't seem to have any effect. Her aunt was working herself up into another bout of hysterics. Desperate, Sidonie racked her brains for what she could say that might calm her down. Tante Josephine didn't understand nuances, and Sidonie knew that if she tried to placate her with reassurances that the debts were now in *her* name it would have no effect. Her aunt still believed the debts were hers.

Her aunt only understood *right now*—and right now, she was panicking. Sidonie knew that in her aunt's mind the threat was as real as if *gendarmes* had just turned up to arrest her.

Tante Josephine needed to hear something concrete, even if it was a white lie. 'Okay, look, Jojo—are you listening to me? I need you to listen because I'm going to tell you why you don't have to worry about a thing.'

To Sidonie's relief her aunt stopped crying abruptly at the use of the nickname that had come about when, as a toddler, Sidonie hadn't been able to pronounce Josephine. She hiccuped softly. Sidonie's heart ached for this poor, sweet and innocent woman who did not deserve this stress.

'Jojo, everything is going to be fine…I promise you.'

Unbeknownst to Sidonie, who stood facing away from the view and the open terrace doors, a tall dark shape had approached and stopped.

'But Sidonie…*how*?'

Sidonie could hear the hysteria approaching again and cursed the distance between them. 'I'm not going to let you go through this alone, Jojo, do you hear me? Didn't I promise to do everything in my power to get us out of this mess?'

Her aunt sniffled and Sidonie pressed on, seizing the advantage, knowing how fragile her aunt was mentally.

'You don't have to worry about a thing because I've…'

Sidonie faltered. She'd been about to say she had everything in hand, but she knew that would sound vague to her aunt, so she mentally crossed her fingers, squeezed her eyes shut and said, 'I've met someone, Jojo…and he's really, really rich. One of the richest men in the world. And you won't believe how we met—it was on a plane, and he *owned* the plane.'

Immediately her aunt, who was always enthralled by stories like this, perked up. 'Really, Sidonie? Truly? Is he your boyfriend?'

Sidonie opened her eyes. 'Yes, he is. He's crazy about me. And I've told him all about you and he's promised to take care of everything.'

As much as Sidonie hated using Alexio like this, she knew it would resonate with her aunt, who was simplistically old-fashioned. After her father had bought the apartment for Tante Josephine she'd believed all men had the power to sweep in and make magic happen.

Her aunt's voice quavered, but this time it sounded like relief. 'Oh, Sidonie…I'm so happy… I was so worried—and then when Marcel told me those things and—'

Sidonie cut her off before she could work herself up again and behind her the tall, dark shadow melted away, unnoticed.

'Jojo, don't talk about this to anyone again—and if Marcel says anything just know that you have nothing to worry about.'

Sidonie felt awful, lying like this, but she knew that her

physical presence would reassure her aunt when she got back to Paris. She could then tell her that something had happened with the *'boyfriend'*. The idea was laughable. Alexio was no boyfriend.

'Oh, Sidonie…is he handsome?'

Sidonie felt ashamed, but she was relieved to hear her aunt's natural effervescence return—she loved stories about people meeting and falling in love. Sidonie tried to gloss over the details about Alexio as much as possible, and before her aunt terminated the conversation she made sure to have a chat with one of the supervisors, to warn them that she was particularly vulnerable at the moment. She castigated herself for not thinking of doing it before the holiday.

When she put her phone down she felt drained, but at least happier that Tante Josephine should be okay until the end of her holiday. The supervisor had promised to keep a close watch over her.

Sidonie turned round and her eyes widened when she saw the tall figure of Alexio, standing with his back to her at the railing of the terrace outside. He was dressed in faded jeans and a T-shirt. That feeling of foreboding was back but Sidonie tried to shake it off. And also the sudden fear that he might have heard some of her conversation.

She padded out on bare feet and went to stand beside Alexio at the railing. He didn't look at her. Sidonie forced her voice to be bright. 'Hey, you…I was wondering where you'd got to.'

Alexio was trying to hold in the cold rage that had filled his belly when he'd overheard her poisonous words: *'He's crazy about me…he'll take care of things…'*

Here was the very unpalatable proof that his solicitor had been right to make Alexio question why Sidonie hadn't told him about this before.

Forcing his voice to sound neutral, he asked, 'Who were you on the phone to just now?'

He couldn't look at her. His hands tightened on the railings.

Sidonie was evasive. 'Er…just my aunt. She's away at the moment, on holiday…'

Alexio felt a hard weight settle into his belly. Everything from the moment he'd met her unspooled like a bad film in his mind. All the little moments when she'd appeared shy, naïve, mocked him now.

So this was how she was going to do it: she was going to bide her time, wait to catch him in a weak moment and then launch into her sob story, seducing money out of him. And maybe even more. Maybe he'd be so weak by then he'd offer to buy her a place, set up her and her aunt completely? He felt dizzy at the thought.

He thought of how weak he'd felt in the aftermath of their lovemaking—how he'd blithely allowed himself to spill his guts, how he'd almost spilled *more*, telling her everything. How close he'd come to making a complete fool of himself.

Thank goodness he'd had the sense to investigate her. When he thought of how guilty he'd felt to have instigated such a thing, the conversation he'd heard just now taunted him. Where had his cynical shell gone?

Sidonie touched his arm. 'What is it, Alexio? You're scaring me.'

Alexio jerked his arm from her as if burnt and stepped back, finally looking at her. He saw her go pale and welcomed it. He couldn't hide his disgust and despised the way his body reacted to seeing her in short shorts and that sexy halterneck top.

'You really think I'm that stupid?' he sneered.

Sidonie looked at him and blinked. He could see something like fear flash in her eyes.

'What did you hear?'

Alexio felt murderous now, because her guilt was obvious.

'Enough,' he spat out. 'Enough to know that you and your aunt think that you can use *me* to clear your debts.'

Sidonie just stood there, looking a little shell-shocked. No doubt because she'd been found out.

She said faintly, 'You speak French.'

'Of course I speak French—along with two or three other European languages.'

He was dismissive.

Sidonie's eyes seemed to clear and she reached out with a hand that Alexio stepped back from. 'You don't understand. I didn't mean a word of it. I was just saying what I could to reassure her—she was upset.'

Alexio could have laughed at her earnest expression, which was a travesty now that he knew everything was twisted and black and nothing had been real. He felt betrayed, and that made him even more incandescent with rage. He *never* let women get close enough to do this to him.

'You expect me to believe a single word from the daughter of a criminal? You obviously learnt well from her— but not well enough. If you had had the decency to *tell* me about this—come to me and merely asked me for help—I might have given it. Instead you insisted on this elaborate charade. Maybe you got off on the drama?'

CHAPTER SEVEN

FOR AN AWFUL second Sidonie thought she might faint. She couldn't actually believe that Alexio had just said those words...*daughter of a criminal.*

She went icy cold, despite the heat, and forced words out through numb lips. 'What do you mean, the daughter of a criminal?'

His voice flat, he admitted, 'I know all about your mother, Sidonie. I know that she blackmailed her married lover and went to jail.'

The words fell like shattered glass all over her. The old shame rose up to grip her vocal cords so she couldn't speak, much in the same way as had happened when she'd been eight years old in the schoolyard and her classmates had surrounded her, jeering, *'Your mother's going to jail...your mother's going to jail...'*

Sidonie could not believe she was hearing this. It had to be a nightmare. Perhaps any minute now she'd wake up to Alexio saying, *Sid...wake up. I want you.*

She blinked. But nothing changed. Alexio was still standing there. A stranger. Cold and remote. Condemnatory. She felt dazed, confused.

Somehow she managed to get out, 'How on earth do you know about that?' Something else struck her. 'And how do you know about my aunt's debts?'

Alexio crossed his arms and now he looked completely forbidding. 'I had you investigated.'

This information made Sidonie literally reel. She had to put her hands behind her on the railing just to hold onto something or she was afraid she'd fall down.

'You had me *investigated*?' she whispered incredulously, looking at him, at this complete stranger.

Alexio lifted one shoulder minutely and didn't look remotely ashamed or sheepish. 'I can't be too careful… Someone, a complete stranger, comes into my life… I got suspicious.'

'My God,' Sidonie breathed, horrified. 'Who *are* you?'

She felt sick. And then angry. It was a huge surge of emotion, rising up within her. She stood up straight, let go of the railing. She was shaking.

'And how *dare* you pry into my private life? What my mother did has got absolutely nothing to do with you.'

Sidonie had lived with that shame all her life but had finally come to terms with what her mother had done—not least because she understood a little of why she'd acted the way she had. Something that she could never explain to this cold stranger. She hadn't even let her guard down enough with him to tell him of her deep private secrets. He'd gone looking for them.

Sidonie was aware of parts of herself breaking off inside, shattering. She knew she had to hold it together.

Alexio spoke again, his voice as cutting as a knife. 'But it wasn't just that, was it? She put your aunt into severe debt, to fund her own expensive tastes.'

Shame heaped on top of shame. Sidonie felt horribly exposed. From somewhere deep inside, and far too late, she reached for and pulled up an icy shield.

'That is none of your concern.' Because she'd never intended to tell him about it. It was part of the real world, which *wasn't* part of this fantasy world.

Alexio's mouth twisted. 'But it would have been, wouldn't it? You were waiting for the right moment, when enough intimacy had been established, and then you were going to make your move. I just wonder if you were going to ask only for enough to cover the debts or more...based on how many nights we'd spent together? Based on how duped you thought I was by then?'

'Theos.' He was lashing out now, making Sidonie flinch. He narrowed wild-looking eyes on her.

'You were good. I'll give you that. But there were a few signs... The way you were so blasé with the clothes, as if you had expected nothing less. That little wistful moment outside the jewellery shop... Were you hoping to wake up and find a diamond bracelet winking at you on the pillow?'

Sidonie desperately tried not to let the awful insidious insecurity take hold, telling her that despite everything she *was* her mother's daughter. Had something about the sheer level of Alexio's wealth called to her? More than the man himself? Suddenly she doubted herself. She had to take deep breaths to avoid throwing up right there on the terrace.

The sheer depth and evidence of Alexio's cynicism was astounding, shocking. The lengths he'd gone to because he hadn't really trusted her... Because he'd *suspected* something.

The things he'd found out... The fact that she had so fatally misread this man. *How* had she not seen an inkling of this? Only those most fleeting moments when a look would cross his face...hardly enough to make her wonder.

Nevertheless, a small, tender part of Sidonie not lashed by this terrible revelation was making her say, 'You have it all wrong. I was only telling my aunt something to re-assure her. She was hysterical. I didn't mean it. You were never meant to hear that and I had no intention of asking you for money.'

To Sidonie's own ears it sounded flat. Didn't sound convincing. She couldn't seem to drum up the necessary passion to convince him. She was too stunned, too shocked… too wounded.

Predictably, Alexio didn't believe her. His eyes were a dead, emotionless void.

'I do not wish to discuss this any further. We're done here. I am going back to Athens within the hour. If you come with me I will ensure you get a flight home.'

Sidonie felt devoid of all feeling except one: she hated this man. And she couldn't believe how gullible she'd been—how naïve not to have assumed that a man as powerful as him would, of course, be suspicious and cynical by nature.

She said flatly, 'I would prefer to swim home.'

Alexio shrugged minutely, as if he couldn't care less. 'As you wish. There's a boat leaving for Piraeus this evening. My housekeeper's husband will take you to the port.'

Sidonie welcomed that. Because right now she hated herself for automatically thinking about what it would be like to get on a plane again without this man distracting her from her fear with his charming sexy smile. With that wicked mouth.

He turned away and then turned back abruptly, his eyes dark. Something in his voice was a bit wild, but Sidonie was too traumatised to notice it.

'Tell me…was it on the plane, when you knew who I was? Did you decide then to try and hook me by making me believe you were different from every other woman I've ever met?'

Sidonie just looked at him. Words of defence were stuck in her throat. She had no defence—not when this man had proved that he had suspected her of something long before he'd even had a reason to. And he still had no reason to. She had trusted him, blindly, right from the start, never suspecting for a moment how dark he was inside. How he could so easily condemn her.

She never wanted to see him again because he had just proved that she would never be free of the past. He had broken her heart into a million pieces and she'd never forgive herself for that weakness. Or him.

His condemnation would be her defence, so she said, 'Yes. On the plane. As soon as I knew who you were.'

Alexio looked at her for a taut moment and then he turned and strode away, leaving her standing there. As soon as he was out of sight Sidonie blindly made her way into the *en suite* bathroom of the bedroom where they'd made love too many times to count and was violently ill.

Afterwards, when Alexio's helicopter had left and she'd changed into her own clothes and packed her bag, Sidonie sat on a lounger outside with the glorious view unnoticed in front of her. She was still numb. Devoid of any substantial feeling. She knew it was the protection of shock.

One thing impinged, though: disgust at herself for having indulged in this fantasy. She'd wanted one night and had then grabbed for more… Had she on some level hoped that Alexio would want her for longer? Deeper? Had she ignored her own usually healthy self-protective cautious nature because she'd been blinded by opulence? The thought made her feel sick again.

Bitterly she surmised that she should have listened to him more closely when he'd told her his reasons for turning his back on his inheritance. He was driven and ruthless—had dashed his own father's expectations and dreams to fuel his own desires.

She'd believed his reasons were justified when she'd heard them at first—she'd heard the way his voice had constricted when he'd talked about his father, as if even now he felt the unbearable yoke of expectation. She'd admired him.

But now she saw him for what he really was: an amoral, ambitious, greedy man who would step over his nearest and dearest to get ahead. She hadn't stood a chance. He might have heard her damning conversation with her aunt, but he'd already investigated her at that stage and had clearly believed her worthy of judgement because of her mother's criminal record.

Those two years of her mother's incarceration were etched like an invisible tatoo into Sidonie's skin. A stain of shame that would never be gone, but which had faded over time…until now.

Sidonie's well-ingrained sense of responsibility rose up. She should never have indulged herself like this. She had her aunt to worry about now, and clearing the debts.

She heard a car pull up somewhere nearby. It would be the housekeeper's husband. She stood up and tried not to let the emotion brewing within her break free. She couldn't let it. She was afraid of its awesome power. Of how much it would tell her about a hurt that shouldn't be so deep—not after just a few days with a man she hadn't even known.

A man appeared, old and bent, with a weathered face and black eyes. His dour expression gave Sidonie some sense of relief. If he'd been kind she might have broken apart altogether. He took her bag and at the same time handed her a white envelope with nothing written on it.

Sidonie opened it and saw a cheque with her name on it inside. It was for an amount of money that took her breath away. Enough to halve her aunt's debts at least. The signature at the bottom was bold and arrogant. Reeking of condemnation and disgust.

Fire filled Sidonie's belly. She stalked straight back into the villa and went to Alexio's office.

She took the cheque out of the envelope and ripped it

up into tiny pieces. Then she put them back in the envelope and wrote on the outside.

It was never about the money.

And then she left.

Four months later...

Alexio looked down at the craggy dark island below him with its distinctive white and blue roofs. The helipad on his own villa loomed into view and tension made his gut hard. Alexio grimaced as his solicitor's words came back to him. *'You're heading for burnout, man. I've never seen you like this before.'*

Alexio couldn't remember being like this before either—not even in the days when he'd been struggling and working night and day to make a success of his business. But for the last four months he'd barely stopped to breathe. On automatic pilot.

His fortune had doubled. His acquisitions had extended to North America, making him the first European budget airline to secure such a lucrative contract. Now he was global, having taken half the time people had predicted.

But Alexio felt as if an essential fire inside him had been doused. He rejected the thought immediately. Nothing was different. He was still the same—held the same values and ambitions.

As the small aircraft circled lower and lower he fought *her* memory. This was precisely why he'd avoided coming back here before now. During daylight hours he had to make a concerted effort not to think of her; that was where work came in. But in the nights she haunted him. Stopped him from sleeping. Made his body ache so badly that he had to ease it like a horny teenager.

He wouldn't mind if he could alleviate his frustration with another woman, but he could barely look at a woman these days without feeling a measure of disgust. And a disturbingly flatlining libido.

He told himself it was because he'd come so close to being burnt. A vivid memory came into his mind as the glittering sun-kissed sea below the villa came into view— Sidonie launching herself onto his back as they'd walked up the steps from the sea, kissing his neck, joking, laughing. And all the time plotting to feather her nest.

Alexio felt sick, and he almost told the pilot to keep going...but they were landing now and Alexio refused to let a memory override his intellect.

He'd finally agreed to go somewhere for a few days' R&R after he and his brother had almost come to blows for the first time in years. Alexio had been closing a deal with Rafaele to create a joint company which would invest in research for future technologies in cars and aircraft. They'd been in Rafaele's *palazzo* outside Milan, where he was spending the summer with his family.

Alexio had been keen to keep working one day and Rafaele had looked at him incredulously. 'Are you crazy? We've been working all day—Sam is making dinner tonight and Milo's back from summer school in Milan. I haven't seen him since this morning. I have a family now, Alexio... things are different.'

Alexio had felt a completely irrational anger erupt at his brother's very valid reasons not to keep working. Since he'd arrived he'd found the domestic idyll of Rafaele's family almost too much to bear. The openly loving looks between him and his wife. His precocious and gorgeous nephew, who bathed everyone in his sunny charming nature. The way he was doted on by both Sam and Rafaele. The way Rafaele's relationship with his own father had clearly undergone a transformation for the better.

It had brought Alexio back to that dark place when he'd believed such things existed, only to find out that they didn't. It had brought back the resentment that he'd felt because he'd witnessed something ugly in his own family that Rafaele had never had to witness simply because he'd been free to get on with his own life, leaving Alexio behind in a toxic atmosphere.

He'd been caught in the grip of that darkness, emotions swirling in his gut, and he'd sneered, 'You're losing your touch, Rafaele, ever since you let that woman get to you—'

His brother had stepped right up to him, chest to chest, and Alexio had felt the heat of his anger.

Rafaele had blistered at him, 'Do not ever call Sam *that woman* again. Whatever is going on with you, Alexio, sort it out.'

Sam had come into the study then, smiling widely, oblivious to the tension at first. And then her grey eyes had grown wide and concerned as she'd immediately looked to her husband. Something in that look, something that had seemed so naked and *dangerous* to Alexio, had made him push past his brother.

He'd found the wherewithal to stop and say tightly, 'I'm sorry, Sam. I have to leave. Something's come up...' and then he'd left the *palazzo* as if hounds were at his heels. Running from that picture of domestic bliss which he wanted to believe was a sham...but which he knew deep down wasn't.

He'd avoided the repeated phone calls from his brother since then.

He was here now, so he'd get it together if it killed him. And maybe tonight he'd go to that nightclub and his libido *wouldn't* flatline in the presence of other women. Maybe it would surge back to life and he would finally be able to erase *her* image from his mind once and for all, claw back some sense of equilibrium.

* * *

Sidonie gave a groan of satisfaction as she slid into the steaming water of the cracked and discoloured bath. Tante Josephine had squirted in enough bubbles to hide Sidonie's body from view completely, but she didn't need it to be hidden to know what she'd see without the bubbles: a small bump protruding over the waterline, as it had started to do over the last week.

It seemed to be getting bigger by the day now as she became more noticeably pregnant.

Her boss at the café had pulled her aside earlier and said bluntly, 'I have five children. You're pregnant, aren't you?'

Sidonie had blanched, too shocked to deny it, and nodded her head.

Her boss had sighed. 'Okay, you can stay for a couple of months, but as soon as you start to get big you're gone—this is not work for a pregnant woman.'

Sidonie had gasped, but he'd walked away. She'd realised the irony of her boss being a chauvinistic Greek man but hadn't felt like laughing.

She bit her lip now with worry. So far she and Tante Josephine were doing okay. When Sidonie had got back to Paris and moved in with her aunt she'd gone to see a financial advisor who had helped them consolidate their debts to a monthly total. Now all Sidonie had to do was earn enough to make that payment. Every month. For a long, long time into the future.

They were just about managing, with Tante Josephine's job and Sidonie's two and sometimes three jobs. But now that a baby was in the mix…

Sidonie bit down on her lip hard and put her hand over the small swell. Since the moment she'd seen the first pregnancy test turn positive, and then the next and the next—five tests in all—she'd forged an indelible bond with the clump of cells growing inside her. She'd never consciously thought about having a baby—it was something she'd put off into the distant future, not really wanting to consider the huge responsibility, especially after her own damaging experiences—but crazily, in spite of everything, somehow it felt *right*. And Sidonie couldn't explain why, when she had every reason to feel the opposite.

Sometimes, though, panic gripped her so hard she had to stop and breathe. She fought it. She would get through this somehow.

It didn't help that Tante Josephine kept asking Sidonie, 'But where is your boyfriend? The one you told me about? Won't he want to take care of you? I thought he was going to make everything okay?'

Sidonie would take her aunt's face in her hands and say firmly, but lovingly, 'We don't need him, Jojo, we have each other. We're a team and we're invincible. I won't let anything happen to us, okay?'

Her aunt would sigh and then quickly get distracted by something—usually talk of the baby. She'd already decided that if it was a boy it would be called Sebastian and if it was a girl Belle, after a favourite cartoon character.

As Sidonie lay in the bath now, after a punishing day of work, she felt helpless tears spring into her eyes. Immediately she cut off the emotion ruthlessly, as she'd been doing for four months. Anger rose and she welcomed it. She cultivated it. It was the only thing that kept her sane, kept her going. And now the baby.

She would never contact *him* and she had to stop thinking about *him*. For a man who had accused her of being a gold-digger on the basis of conducting an investigation into her private life and overhearing an admittedly unfortunate conversation, news of a baby would consign her to the hell of his condemnation for good—and she would not give him the satisfaction.

Her anger rose, swift and bright, washing away those

dangerous tender feelings that hovered on the periphery and had no place after what he'd done to her.

Alexio returned to the villa feeling more disgruntled than ever. After sleeping for almost eight hours on a lounger on the terrace he'd gone to the club.

Elettra, encouraged by the fact that he was alone, had twined herself around him like a clinging vine, making him feel nothing but claustrophobia.

In a fit of darkness he'd taken the same booth as last time and had been bombarded with images and memories: Sidonie's dress, the way the silk had clung and moved with her body. How it had felt to dance close to her, sliding his hand under her dress to touch her naked back. The insistent throb of the music, with the same beat as the desire rushing through his blood. The way she'd looked at him, hungry and innocent.

Innocent.

Except she'd never been innocent. She'd been scheming the whole time, just reeling him in, waiting for an opportunity to secure her future, debt-free.

Bile had risen up inside Alexio after all these months, just as it had that awful day. Immediately he'd had to get out of there.

And now here he was, looking over the inky blackness of the sea. Thoroughly disgusted with himself, Alexio felt the lure of work—even though he meant to be avoiding it. But he knew he wouldn't sleep, and especially not in that bed. It had been a terrible idea to come here. He should have gone to the farthest corner of the world and he vowed to do so the next day. He'd wanted to check out the potential of setting up in South East Asia anyway…

When he went into the office and sat down heavily on the chair he saw an unexpected white envelope sitting squarely on the blotter. Saw the writing in a feminine scrawl.

It was never about the money.

Feeling something in his belly swoop and his skin prickle, Alexio picked up the envelope. As he did so something fluttered out. The torn pieces of the cheque he'd left for Sidonie in a fit of tumultuous anger and disgust. If she wanted the money so badly then he'd give her some. But now he felt dizzy. Disorientated. He opened the envelope and more and more pieces fell out. Nothing else.

It was never about the money.

He hadn't even checked to see if or when she'd cashed it. He'd just assumed that she had. He hadn't wanted to know. But she hadn't. She'd left that day and taken a torturous eleven-hour ferry to Piraeus. His last contact from her had been via a message relayed to him by one of his Greek assistants whom he'd instructed to meet her at the port with a plane ticket for a flight to Dublin.

She'd not taken the ticket and had said succinctly, *'Tell Alexio Christakos he can go to hell.'*

The message had been relayed with great trepidation by the employee after Alexio had instructed him to tell him her words *exactly*.

Alexio had put it down to anger that he'd thwarted her plans. He'd felt vindicated. But now he felt sick. Why hadn't she just taken the cheque?

Holding the jagged remains made a conflicting mix of things rush through him. Not least of which was the poisonous suspicion that this was a desperate ruse to pique his interest—make him go after her to find out *why*. So that ultimately she might get even more money.

Even now Alexio could feel anticipation spiking in his blood just at the thought of seeing her again, but...*damn her*...had she counted on this?

He felt something underneath him then, and shifted slightly to find that he was sitting on Sidonie's tatty university sweatshirt. She must have left it behind that day. Her pale face and wide, stricken eyes came back to him— the way she'd flatly agreed with him that, *yes*, she'd set out to seduce him on the plane. Something about that felt off now. His gut twisted...

She had protested her innocence. But he'd been so incensed he'd been unable to feel anything but the bitter sting of betrayal and anger at his own weakness for her.

Emotion, hot and impossible to push down, made his chest go tight. Without even thinking about what he was doing he brought the sweatshirt up to his nose and breathed deeply. Her scent, still faint but there, hit him like a steam train, that intriguing mix between floral and something spiky.

Galvanised by something that felt like a combination of panic and desperation, Alexio stood up and went into the bedroom. He hadn't opened the closet doors yet but now he did. All of the clothes were still hanging there. The clothes that he had ordered to be delivered for Sidonie before they'd arrived. She'd taken nothing. Not even the dress she'd worn to the club that night.

He could hear her voice as if she was there right now: *'Well, at least I won't have to worry about washing my knickers out in the sink. I'm sure your housekeeper would be horrified.'* This time Alexio heard and recognised the over-brightness of her voice and his sense of discomfort grew.

'You'll have to do it again. It's not good enough.'

Sidonie fought down the urge to scream and smiled as if her boss *wasn't* a sadistic control freak. There was nothing wrong with the way she'd made this bed in the five-star hotel where she worked for minimum wage three days a week.

'No problem.'

'And please hurry—the guest is due to arrive within the hour.'

Sidonie sighed deeply and stripped the bed in order to make it again. She ached all over and she longed for a hot bath like the one she'd had the other night. She hadn't had the time since then, because she'd taken on a full-time waitressing job in a Moroccan restaurant near the apartment six evenings a week. Her boss there had no qualms about hiring a pregnant woman, unlike the boss of the café where she worked the other two days a week when she wasn't at the hotel.

Finally her shift was over and she stretched out her back, instinctively putting a hand over her small bump, feeling the prickle of guilt. She knew she shouldn't be working so hard but she had no choice. A small voice taunted her. *You could contact him.* But she slammed her locker door shut in the staff changing room.

No way. Not going there. The thought of crawling to Alexio for help was anathema. She never wanted to see his cold, judgmental face again.

But when she emerged from the staff entrance at the side of the hotel and walked to the top of the lane his was the first face she saw. Shock held her immobile. He was leaning nonchalantly against the bonnet of a gleaming sports car, with his hands in his trouser pockets and his legs crossed at the ankles. Then he saw her and tensed, straightened up.

She blinked, but he didn't disappear. He was looking right at her with those golden-green eyes. For an awful treacherous second emotion rose in a dizzying sweep inside Sidonie. Her blood grew hot in her veins and her breath shortened. Her nipples tingled. All the signs of a woman in the throes of a lust that had lain dormant.

The oppressive, muggy August air seemed to seize the oxygen going into her lungs. For a second she felt so light-headed she thought she'd faint and she sucked in breath. It couldn't be him, she told herself, in spite of his not disappearing. It was a mirage. An apparition from her imagination torturing her.

In a bid to convince herself of that Sidonie turned and started to walk down the street. She heard a curse behind her and then her arm was taken in a strong grip. A familiar grip. Immediately Sidonie reacted violently to the effect it had on her body and soul and whirled around, ripping herself free.

She looked up and felt dizzy again. It was Alexio. In the flesh. That gorgeous flesh. He had no right to look so gorgeous. She frowned. Even if he did look leaner than when she'd last seen him and even if there were lines around his mouth and face. Lines she recognised, because she saw them in her own mirror every day. But he was still gorgeous, and she was still aware of the woman who had just walked past and done a double-take.

Anger flared and she seized it like a drowning person might seize a buoy.

'What do you want?' she spat out, her belly jumping with panic and a mix of other things she didn't want to investigate.

Sidonie vaguely noticed his open-necked light blue shirt and dark trousers and became very belatedly aware of her own woeful state of dress. Skinny jeans which she had to wear with the button open, flip-flops and a loose sleeveless smock shirt. Panic gripped her and then she reassured herself. He wouldn't notice the bump.

The fact that he hadn't come looking for her sooner stung her more than she liked to admit. She was pathetic.

That hatred burned bright within her, giving her strength. 'Well? What do you want? As far as I recall I didn't take anything on my way out of the villa.'

'No,' Alexio said heavily, 'it's what you left behind.'

Sidonie went blank for a moment, and then she saw that cheque in her mind's eye and felt fury all over again. Suddenly it made sense and she said out loud, 'You went back to the villa and discovered I hadn't cashed your precious cheque?'

'Yes,' he admitted.

Sidonie didn't like the way that made the fury diminish slightly. She'd assumed that he'd known all along that she hadn't taken his money and that it had made no difference. But all this time he'd thought she'd cashed in. Still, that didn't change anything.

'And this...'

Sidonie looked to see him holding out her university sweatshirt and was immediately bombarded with memories of meeting him on that plane, feeling like a hick.

She took it from him and said cuttingly, 'You came all this way to deliver my sweatshirt?'

A muscle in his jaw popped and Sidonie felt increasingly vulnerable.

She looked at her watch, and then at him, and injected her voice with false sweetness. 'Look, I'd love to stay and chat, but I have work to get to—so if you don't mind...'

She turned to walk away but he caught her arm again and Sidonie's blood leapt. She stopped and turned around and said in a low voice, 'Let me go, Christakos. We have nothing to say to each other.'

Except for the fact that he's the father of the baby growing in your belly.

Sidonie ignored her conscience. She needed to get away from him before her composure slipped.

Alexio battled to control the lust that had almost felled him the second he'd laid eyes on Sidonie again. His libido was back with a vengeance. He felt the fragility of Sidonie's arm under his hand. She'd lost weight—weight

she could ill afford to lose. Her face was more angular...
giving it a haunting beauty. Her eyes looked huge and
there were shadows underneath. She was exhausted. He
recognised it well.

He frowned. 'Aren't you just leaving work?'

She tried to pull her arm out of his grip but he had an
almost visceral fear that if he let her go he'd never see her
again. That glorious light golden hair was duller than he
remembered, and scooped up into a bun much as it had
been when they'd first met. Her neck looked long and
vulnerable.

'I have two jobs—daytime and evening. Now, if you
don't mind, I don't want to be late.'

'I'll give you a lift,' Alexio said impulsively.

He was still trying to get his head around seeing her
again. His conscience pricked hard. She hadn't taken the
money and she was working two jobs. To pay off the debts.
Debts that weren't even hers. Because she had never wanted
the money from him in the first place. The ramifications
of this, if it were true, made Alexio reel.

This time Sidonie wrenched her arm free. She glared
at Alexio and her eyes spat blue and green sparks at him.
'No, thank you. I do not want a lift or anything else from
you. Now, please, go back to where you came from and
leave me be.'

She turned and hurried away, her bag slung over her
body. She looked very young. Alexio was grim. No way
was he going to walk away until he knew what she was up
to. The fact that he was clearly the last person she wanted
to see only made him more determined.

As Alexio battled not to go and grab her again, and
watched her disappear down the steps of a nearby metro
station, he took out his mobile phone and made a terse call.

CHAPTER EIGHT

THAT NIGHT WHEN Sidonie left the Moroccan restaurant she felt so weary she could have cried. It wasn't helped by the state of agitation she'd been in all day after seeing Alexio. She'd kept expecting him to pop up out of nowhere again and she couldn't forget how he'd looked so drawn. Intense. He hadn't looked like the carefree playboy she remembered.

Still… She firmed her mouth. She'd done the right thing by sending him away. He had no right to come barging into her life again just because he wanted to solve the riddle of the mysterious uncashed cheque.

She would never forgive him for delving into her private life, seeking out her most painful memory and then throwing it in her face as an accusation. He hadn't been remotely interested in listening to her protest her innocence because he'd been all too ready to believe she was just as guilty as her mother. Although Sidonie winced slightly when she thought of the misfortune of him hearing that phone call when he had.

As Sidonie approached Tante Josephine's apartment she saw a familiar low-slung vehicle parked outside. Clearly out of place in this run-down area of Paris.

Her heart thumped erratically. The car was empty. Sidonie looked up and could see the first-floor apartment's lights blazing. Tante Josephine was usually in bed by now. Sidonie had a horrific image of her beloved Jojo being confronted by a tall, dark, intimidating Alexio and stumbled in her haste to get in.

When she almost fell in the front door she saw an idyllic scene of domesticity. Her Tante Josephine was perched on the edge of a chair, holding a cup of tea, and Alexio was seated opposite her on the couch, drinking a cup of coffee.

Tante Josephine put down her cup and stood up, her small matronly bosom quivering with obvious excitement. Her cheeks were bright pink. Sidonie could have rolled her eyes in disgust. The Alexio charm offensive had struck again.

Her aunt took her hands as she came in and Sidonie shot an accusing look at Alexio, whose face was unreadable. But something in his eyes made her heart jump. It was dark. Hard. As it had been on that day.

'Oh, Sidonie, your friend called by earlier. I told him he could wait here for you and we've been having the most pleasant chat.'

Alexio stood up then and made the small apartment laughably smaller. He looked pointedly at her belly and said, in perfect accentless French, 'I believe congratulations are in order?'

Sidonie went cold. *No.* Her aunt couldn't have… But she was notoriously indiscreet—especially with strangers…

Sidonie looked at her with horrified eyes but Tante Josephine, having the nous to suspect that something had just gone very wrong, fluttered nervously and said, 'Well, it's past my bedtime. I'll leave you young people to catch up.'

And then she was gone, leaving Sidonie facing her nemesis. The air was thick with tension.

Sidonie lifted her chin and waited. It didn't take long.

'You're pregnant?'

She tried not to be intimidated by the murderous look on Alexio's face. She'd never allowed herself the indulgence of daydreaming about this scenario, but for a man who didn't even want *a relationship*, this was pretty close to what she might have imagined.

'Yes,' she confirmed starkly, reluctantly. 'I'm pregnant.'

Alexio went pale under his olive skin. His voice sounded rough. 'Whose is it?'

Sidonie gaped at him. She'd also never envisaged that he would doubt the baby was his. She started to speak but a flash of anger rendered her speechless again. Incensed, she stalked over to him and planted her hands on her hips, looked up into that remote hard-boned face.

'Well,' she said, her voice dripping with sarcasm, 'I *did* have a threesome shortly after you cast me out of your life like a piece of unwanted luggage, so it could be Tom, Dick or Harry's baby. But we won't know until it's born and we can see who she or *he* looks like.' She was breathing hard.

Alexio just looked at her.

Growing even more incensed, Sidonie stabbed at his chest with her finger and tried to ignore how hard it felt.

'It's yours, you arrogant jerk,' she hissed, mindful of Tante Josephine. 'Cold-bloodedly seducing another billionaire hasn't exactly been high on my priority list lately.'

Alexio looked down into that furious face and felt numb. He welcomed it. His solicitor had failed to mention the very poignant fact that Sidonie's aunt had mild mental health issues.

And now…now *the baby*. *His* baby. Ever since Tante Josephine had excitedly informed him that Sidonie was expecting a baby, Alexio had felt as if he'd swallowed nails.

At first he'd told himself it couldn't possibly be his: they'd used protection every time. He'd been fanatical about it. Except for when they'd come home from the club and made love in the car, unable even to walk the few steps into the villa. That night was almost sixteen weeks ago now. Sixteen weeks of living in a blur. And now suddenly everything was in focus again.

Disgust at the memory of his lack of control that night had curdled his insides as Sidonie's aunt had chattered on, blithely unaware of the bomb she'd dropped. And then Sidonie had come in, looking panicked. Guilty.

The knowledge that she was telling the truth sank into him like a stone, casting huge ripples outward. He wanted to walk out through the door and keep walking. The sum of all his fears was manifesting itself right now in this room. He wasn't anywhere near ready to contemplate bringing a child into the world. Not after the childhood he'd endured.

A child had perhaps existed in his future life—far in the distant future—along with his perfect blonde wife. He had vowed long ago to make sure that no child of his would see the ugly reality of marriage, because any union *he* would have would be a union of respect and affection—not one punctuated by cold silences, bitter rows, possessive jealousy and violence.

'Well?' Sidonie demanded, hands on hips. 'Aren't you going to say something?'

Alexio's gaze narrowed on her and he realised he wanted to say plenty—but most of it involved his mouth being on Sidonie's. And then his gaze travelled down and he saw the small proud bump evident under her light jacket and the black clingy top she wore. Something within him seemed to break apart. Crumble.

Her hand went there automatically, as if to protect the child, and Alexio felt incensed at that. He thought of the recent revelation of the existence of his oldest half-brother and how his mother had kept him a dirty secret. After abandoning him. Would Sidonie have kept this child from him?

Finally he found his voice, and it was accusing. 'Why didn't you come to me?'

* * *

Sidonie let out a small mirthless laugh and backed away a step. Standing this close to Alexio was hazardous to her mental health and to her libido, which had decided to come out of its ice-like state.

She'd been dreadfully sick for the first trimester of her pregnancy but thankfully that had stopped and she was finally beginning to feel human again. She did not welcome this resurgence of a desire she had no control over.

Alexio was looking increasingly explosive as the news sank in and Sidonie felt a twinge of conscience. She recalled her own shock at finding out about the pregnancy, four weeks after she'd come back to Paris and with no sign of her period.

She crossed her arms tightly. 'You really think I would come to you with this news after you accused me of being a gold-digger? After you judged and tried me—after you had me *investigated* like a common criminal?'

Alexio flushed. 'Why did you agree with me, then, and let me believe that you set out to seduce me?'

Sidonie's arms tightened. 'I told you the truth, but you weren't interested in listening. Would you have believed me if I'd insisted on protesting my innocence?'

Remembering the excoriating feeling of betrayal was acute. Sidonie's emotions were rising and she knew she was too tired to hide them. She stood back and gestured to the door.

'I'd like you to leave now, please. I have to be up early.'

Alexio's eyes widened; his nostrils flared. He looked huge and intimidating, and Sidonie hated the impulse she had to run into his arms and beg him to hold her. She gritted her jaw and avoided his eyes.

Silkily he said, 'You expect me to just walk away?'

Sidonie nodded. 'Yes, please. We have nothing to discuss. You found me, I'm pregnant—end of story. You have nothing else to do here. Please go.'

Alexio's voice was tight with anger. 'We have plenty to discuss if I am your child's father. And you still haven't told me why you didn't take the money.'

Sidonie rounded on him again, eyes blazing, two spots of pink in each cheek. 'I didn't take your damn money, Christakos, because I wasn't interested in your money. I wasn't then and I'm not now.'

Emotion was getting the better of Sidonie, rising, making her shake.

'I will never forgive you for going behind my back and prying into my life. You had no right to judge me on the basis of something my mother did years ago. She paid that due, *I* paid that due, and so did my father. I want nothing to do with you and I wish I'd never laid eyes on you.'

She turned and went to the door, opened it.

Without looking at Alexio she said, 'I have to be up in five hours. Get out or I'll call the police and tell them you're harassing me.'

Alexio made some sort of sound—half anger, half frustration. To Sidonie's everlasting relief, though, he came to the door. She didn't look at him.

He said, with deadly precision, 'This isn't over, Sidonie. We need to talk.'

'Get out, Alexio.' Sidonie's voice had an edge of pleading to it that she hated. But finally he left.

For three days Sidonie had refused to talk to Alexio. She stonewalled him if he was waiting for her to come out of the hotel. She walked in the opposite direction if he was there when she emerged from the café. And at night she was tight-lipped if he offered her a lift for the short distance to the apartment after finishing her shift in the Moroccan restaurant.

Alexio seethed with frustration. He was getting her message loud and clear. She wanted nothing to do with him. She preferred working herself into a lather doing menial jobs rather than turn to him for help. But Alexio had had enough. He'd already set things in motion. Sidonie was pregnant with his child and that changed everything. As he'd watched her for the past three days the knowledge had sunk in more and more.

He needed to talk to her, though. And even though she looked half dead with exhaustion Alexio's body burned for her. Even now, from his car, where he was parked outside the restaurant, he let his gaze rake her up and down, taking in the black skirt, sheer tights and black top. The apron that barely disguised the growing swell of her belly. *His baby.*

In the past few days he'd had time for the news of the baby to sink in, and much to his surprise he'd found himself *not* feeling as trapped as he might have expected. Instead he felt a fledgling sense of excitement, wonder.

He thought of his nephew Milo and wondered if he'd have a son too—precocious and cute like him. Or a daughter, like Sidonie, with golden hair? When he imagined that he felt a tightening sensation in his chest so strong he had to take deep breaths to ease it.

She was serving a big table of men now, and she plucked the pen out from where she'd stuck it into the bun on the top of her head. She looked tired and harassed. Pale.

Alexio saw one of the men put a fleshy hand on her arm and a red mist came over his vision. Before he'd even realised what he was doing he was out of the car and pushing open the door of the small tatty restaurant.

'Sir,' Sidonie gritted out, 'please take your hand off me.'

'Don't tell me what to do. You're serving *me.*'

Sidonie felt a frisson of fear cutting through her hazy exhaustion, but even that didn't give her enough adrenalin to pull free. Just then a blast of warm evening air hit Sidonie's back and she looked around automatically to see Alexio, bearing down on her, his face tight with anger, his eyes fixed on where the man still held her.

Her heart thumped unevenly. For three days he'd dogged her heels and she'd ignored him. She'd seen his car outside and had hated to admit to herself that a part of her liked knowing he was there. She'd told herself stoutly that she hoped he was bored to tears and that she'd irritate him so much that he'd leave and never come back.

Alexio was right behind her now, and treacherously she wanted to lean back, to sink against him. That kept her rigid, fighting the waves of weariness which seemed to be gathering force.

His voice came low and threatening over her head.

'Let her go.'

The heavyset man was drunk and belligerent. He tightened his grip on Sidonie's arm, making her gasp out loud. Alexio reached around her and prised the man's fingers off her arm. He drew her back against him, his other hand going around her midriff, where her belly was round.

It was his touch that did it. It burned like a physical brand. It was too much. Alexio was turning her around now, looking down at her, asking something, but she couldn't hear it because a white noise was making her head fuzzy.

As if standing apart from herself, observing, Sidonie saw herself looking utterly fragile and helpless, with Alexio's hands huge on her arms, and she felt a moment of disgust at herself before everything went black.

Sidonie was in a dark, peaceful place with a soft regular *beep-beep* sound coming from somewhere nearby. Slowly, though, as her consciousness returned so did her memory, and she remembered looking up into Alexio's face and seeing him frown.

Alexio.

The baby.

Tante Josephine.

Sidonie's eyes opened and she winced at the bright light and the stark whiteness of the room. She went to move her arm and something pulled. She looked down to see a tube coming out of the back of her hand.

Her head felt slightly woolly. She noticed a movement out of the corner of her eye—something big—and then Alexio loomed into her vision. Tall and dark. His shirt open at the neck, looking crumpled. Stubble on his jaw.

The faint *beep-beep* sound got faster.

Automatically Sidonie's free hand went to her midriff, where she felt the comforting swell of her baby. Even so, she looked at Alexio. 'The baby?'

He looked grim. 'The baby is fine.'

'Tante Josephine?'

'Is fine too. She's been here all night. I sent her home a while ago.'

'All night?'

'You collapsed in the restaurant. I brought you straight to A and E in my car. You've been on a drip since you arrived and unconscious for nearly eight hours.'

'Am I okay?'

Some of the obvious tension left Alexio's jaw. 'The doctor said you're suffering from a mixture of exhaustion and stress and are generally run down.'

'Oh.'

Alexio started to look grim again, making flutters erupt in Sidonie's belly.

'You've run yourself completely into the ground...'

Something dangerous welled up inside her at his obvious censure and she looked away, terrified of the way her throat was starting to hurt and of the emotion which wouldn't go down.

In a voice that was far too high and tight she said, 'Thank you for bringing me here. You can go now.'

Alexio merely walked around the bed until he was in her eyeline again and folded his arms. Succinctly he said, 'No way.'

Just then the door opened and Sidonie turned her head to see a doctor and a nurse come in.

The doctor declared in French, 'You're awake! You gave us a bit of a scare, young lady…'

While he and the nurse did some tests and elaborated on what Alexio had told her Sidonie was busy trying to block out his presence in the room.

The doctor was soon sitting on the side of the bed and saying, 'You're due for your twenty-week scan in a few weeks, but after what's happened I'd like to do a scan now, just so we can double-check everything is okay.'

He must have seen something on her face because he said quickly, 'I've no reason not to believe everything is fine, but we'd like to be sure.'

Within a few minutes Sidonie was being wheeled in her bed to another part of the hospital. Alexio was by her side. She felt panicky. She was about to have a scan with Alexio looking on. She'd never envisaged *this* happening.

After they were wheeled into the room it all happened very fast. Sidonie's belly was bared and they were smoothing cold gel over it. She felt acutely self-conscious all of a sudden—which was crazy considering Alexio had seen more of her naked body than she probably had herself.

When the doctor put the ultrasound device over her belly a rapid sound filled the room. The baby's heartbeat. Immediately Sidonie's focus went to the screen, which was showing a fuzzy grey image. Her heart thumped as emotion climbed upwards again—but this time it was a different kind of emotion.

After a few minutes the doctor smiled and said, 'Everything looks absolutely normal. You have a fine, healthy baby, Sidonie—a little small, but developing well.'

Then he looked at her and at Alexio.

'Would you like to know the sex?' he asked. 'It's quite clear at the moment.'

Sidonie looked at Alexio, mortified that the doctor had assumed they were together. Even if Alexio *was* the father.

Alexio looked inscrutable and then said, 'It's up to you.'

Sidonie wrenched her gaze away from his with more effort than she liked and looked at the doctor again. She said hesitantly, 'I…I think so.' And then more firmly, as a sense of excitement took hold, 'Yes. I'd like to know.'

The doctor beamed at them. 'I'm very pleased to tell you you're having a baby girl.'

Sidonie felt something joyous erupt in her chest and heard a slightly choked sound coming from beside her. She looked up to see Alexio's eyes fixed on the screen, and there was an expression on his face that she'd never seen before. A kind of wonder.

Her belly swooped. She'd never allowed herself to imagine this kind of scenario. She'd expected to have the baby and then see how she felt about informing him, making sure she did it in such a way that he knew she wasn't telling him in order to get his money.

The thought of being likened to her grasping mother again had made her feel sick. But now that had all been taken out of her hands and she had the very uncomfortable sensation that Alexio was about to get a lot more prominent in her life.

Especially when the doctor wiped the gel off her belly, rearranged her clothes and said, 'We'll keep you in for one more night to help you get your strength back, and then I've been assured that your partner here will be getting you the best care and attention until you're back on your feet.'

Sidonie's head swivelled from Alexio's determined expression to the doctor's equally stern-looking face. *Her partner.* The words sent more flutters into her belly. After three days of being followed, she knew the likelihood of shaking Alexio off when she was feeling weak and vulnerable was extremely unlikely.

She looked at Alexio and said, 'I don't have much choice, do I?'

'No,' he agreed equably.

And that was that.

A week later

'You've done *what*?' Sidonie's mind was hot with rage and she felt her heart-rate zooming skyward, the flutters increasing in her belly. She even put a hand there unconsciously, barely noticing how Alexio's eyes dropped to take in the movement. She was too incensed.

Alexio faced her across the expanse of the beautiful first-floor apartment living room, overlooking the Jardin du Luxembourg. He was dressed in a steel-grey shirt and black trousers and Sidonie didn't like the way she was so *aware* of his physicality. The way she became even more aware of it each day as she grew stronger.

Alexio's voice was low, deep, 'I should have known Tante Josephine couldn't keep it quiet. I asked her not to say anything until you'd had a few more days' rest. But I didn't want her to be worried with you out of work.'

Sidonie struggled to take this in—along with the reminder that Alexio and Tante Josephine seemed to have forged a mutual admiration society.

Sidonie had been in this apartment, which Alexio was renting, for almost a week now. A week of Alexio being cool and solicitous. The consummate host. Paying for a nurse to come every day to check on Sidonie. Taking her outside to the Jardin du Luxembourg across the road to get some air. He was seemingly unperturbed by her continued campaign of obdurate silence, which was more due to her wish to avoid this reckoning and his probing gaze than to anything else. Her searing anger had been proving hard to hang onto, as if merely being in his presence on a daily basis was wearing away at it.

Except now it was back, and Sidonie welcomed it.

Her aunt had just left, to be taken home by Alexio's driver, but before she'd gone she'd spilled her secret.

Sidonie had marched straight into Alexio's office without knocking and declared, 'We need to talk.'

He'd looked up from his papers and sat back, arching a brow. '*Now* you're ready to talk?'

Before she'd had time to regret her impetuous action Sidonie had turned on her heel and walked into the vast living room, not liking how intimate the office space had felt. She had also been very aware that his assistant, who was there every day, had left. Until now she'd been a master at staying out of Alexio's way in the spacious apartment.

Sidonie crossed her arms over her chest and almost winced at how sensitive her breasts were. They had grown bigger. That awareness made her voice curt.

'Answer my question.'

Alexio looked as immovable as a rock, tall and intimidating. At that very moment Sidonie had a vivid memory of lying naked beneath him, spreading her legs wide to accommodate his body, feeling the bold thrust of his arousal against her slick body. Her legs wobbled alarmingly but she held firm.

Thankfully Alexio spoke before Sidonie's wayward memory could take over completely.

'I have paid off all of the debts and ensured that your aunt's mortgage has been paid in full.'

The sheer ease with which he'd been able to magic their debts away made her feel disorientated.

'How dare you?'

Sidonie was trembling. But she was afraid it was more to do with his proximity than her anger.

Alexio's eyes narrowed on her. 'I dare because you are carrying my child and we are now family. Tante Josephine is as much my responsibility as you are—and the baby.'

Sidonie's arms grew so tight she could feel her nails digging into her skin. She spoke from a deep well of hurt and rejection at this attempt to muscle into their lives. 'We are not your responsibility. I never came to you. I want nothing from you. As soon as I'm feeling better I will go and find work again and pay you back what we owe.'

Alexio's mouth went into a bitter line. 'I think you've more than proved your point, Sid. You'd prefer to put our child's health in jeopardy in order to save your pride.'

A lurch of hurt emotion rose up, strangling Sidonie for a moment. Then his words *our child* and *Sid* impacted.

When she'd gathered herself she said with quiet ferocity, 'Do not call me that. My name is Sidonie. And the last thing I want to do is put *my* child in danger. I will keep working because, in case you've forgotten, you called me a hustler and I would prefer to work than to be accused of being that again.'

To her horror, Sidonie's voice had cracked on the last words and she turned now, facing blindly away from Alexio, breathing harshly, emotion getting the better of her.

She heard him move behind her and said rawly, 'Don't come near me.'

He stopped. Tears stung at Sidonie's eyes; her throat ached. She hated him. And she repeated this to herself as she struggled to regain her equilibrium.

His voice came from behind her, tight. 'Sidonie, we need to talk about this… I recognise that I was too hasty that day. I didn't give you a chance to explain.'

Sidonie let out a half-choked laugh at that understatement and said bitterly, 'No, you'd obviously made up your mind and couldn't wait to see the back of me.'

She heard him sigh. The shadows outside were lengthening into dusk. His voice was gruffer now. 'The chef has left some food for us. Let's eat and then we can talk…okay?'

Like a coward, she felt herself wanting to make up some excuse, say that she was too tired, but in truth she felt fine. She turned round, arms still crossed, and faced him. His eyes were intense and her skin prickled. She couldn't keep putting off the conversation.

'Okay, fine.'

Within minutes Alexio was serving them both a light chicken casserole in the dining room off the kitchen area. They ate in silence, but tension was mounting inside Sidonie as she tried to avoid looking at Alexio's large hands and remembering how they'd felt on her skin.

Sitting here eating like this was bringing back memories of that first night in London. The sheer fizzing exhilaration of anticipation. And as if her body was some dumb appendage—an assortment of limbs that wasn't attached to her brain—that same fizzing anticipation was rushing through her right now. Gathering force.

She was uncomfortably aware of every erogenous zone. Her breasts felt tender, sensitive. Swollen. She couldn't stop imagining Alexio's mouth lowering towards one thrusting, naked peak…

With a spurt of agitation, Sidonie let her knife drop with a clatter to the plate. Alexio looked up, that gaze narrowed on her flushed face.

Sidonie stood up, feeling feverish. 'I've had enough. Food.' *God.* She couldn't even articulate a sentence.

Alexio looked as cool as a cucumber while Sidonie felt a bead of sweat trickle between her breasts.

He wiped his mouth with his napkin and said, 'Coffee?'

Sidonie seized on the chance to escape that incisive gaze

and nodded her head. 'Some herbal tea, maybe…the house-keeper brought some today.'

Alexio got up and left the room. Cursing herself for this very unwelcome resurgence of desire, Sidonie went back into the drawing room to stand at the window. Praying for control. Praying that the butterflies in her belly would cease.

She put her hand on her belly and was half frowning at how strong the sensation was when she suddenly realised something. She gasped out loud.

A voice came from behind her, concerned. 'What is it?'

Sidonie whirled around, alight with her discovery for a moment, forgetting everything else. 'For a few days I've been feeling butterflies, but I thought it was—'

She stopped dead, because she'd been about to blurt out *just your effect on me.*

She blushed and said, 'It's the baby. I can feel the baby moving…'

Alexio was holding out a cup towards her and she grabbed it before she could see the effect of her words on his face.

She had a sudden image of one of his hands splayed across her belly and said quickly, 'It's not strong enough yet for anyone else to feel…'

Sidonie took the cup and moved away, taking a sip to hide her burning face.

Alexio gritted his jaw at how Sidonie moved so skittishly away from him, that golden hair looking so much shinier and thicker now, down and shielding her face from him. In the space of only a few days of rest and being well fed she was already looking so much better. The hollows of her cheeks were filling out.

He felt as if he was going to snap soon with the tension building inside him. With every second that passed he wanted to turn into a feral animal and strip Sidonie bare and take her, sating himself and drowning out the recriminatory voices in his head.

But he couldn't. She was pregnant. And she hated his guts.

She looked incredibly young now, in leggings and a loose T-shirt. Of course she'd refused his offers to get her some clothes, so her Tante Josephine had brought her some.

When he could finally move his gaze up from those slim shapely legs and over her belly, hidden under the loose material, to her face, she was looking at him with that aquamarine gaze, something determined in their depths.

'Why did you have me investigated?'

Alexio put down his coffee cup onto a nearby table. Sidonie had her hands wrapped tightly around her own mug.

He looked into her eyes. He owed her this.

'Because what happened between us made me nervous. Because I'd never taken a woman to Santorini before. Because for my whole life I've been cynical and when I was with you I forgot to be. And it freaked me out enough to think that by investigating you I'd still be in control.'

CHAPTER NINE

SIDONIE BLINKED. SHE tried to take his words in. Her belly felt as if it was dropping from a height, and she felt unsteady. 'I'm…you hadn't taken a woman there before?'

He shook his head, eyes intent on her reaction.

She couldn't even hide it. She thought of something. 'But…the clothes…I assumed they had belonged to other women…' Sidonie felt very gauche now.

Alexio frowned and then emitted a disgusted, '*Theos.* You think I would do that? Buy a wardrobe full of clothes and just hope that they would fit a stream of women?'

Sidonie glared back at him, stung with embarrassment. 'Well, how would I know? I thought that was some lovers' bolthole.'

Alexio ran a hand through his hair and said, half to himself, 'No wonder you sounded funny…and yet you didn't say anything.'

Now Sidonie was squirming. 'I didn't want to look stupid…or naïve. If you'd had lovers who were used to that kind of thing…'

The clothes had been bought for her alone. The knowledge made her reel. They hadn't been cast-offs. Sidonie felt increasingly as if she wanted to claim fatigue and run away. But Alexio had a familiar stern look on his face now.

Sidonie went and sat down on a nearby couch, placing

her cup on a table. She clasped her hands on her lap to stop them trembling.

Alexio walked away and stood at the window with his back to her for a long moment, as if he too had to gather himself. When he turned around he looked bleak.

'My solicitor had rung me with what he'd learned about your past that day… I told him it had nothing to do with you. But then he told me about the fact that you'd taken on your aunt's debts, and that put a question in my head as to why you hadn't mentioned this—why you were acting as if you didn't have this huge thing hanging over you.'

Sidonie replied, with a trace of bitterness, 'Because I was escaping from it. I never had any intention of telling you about it. What did it have to do with anything? I knew we were only going to be together for a few days…it was only meant to be one night.'

That last came out almost accusingly as Sidonie recalled how persuasive he'd been and how easily she'd capitulated.

'I knew my aunt was okay—she was on holiday with a group she travels with every year…'

Alexio's voice was hard. 'My solicitor put the seed of suspicion in my head. I refused to believe the worst, though. I told him that. I was angry with myself for even asking him to investigate you.' He sighed heavily. 'I went looking for you. I was going to confess what I'd done and ask you about it…and that's when I overheard part of your conversation.'

Sidonie felt as if the wind had been knocked out of her for a moment at hearing this. When she could speak she admitted, 'I can appreciate how damning that conversation must have been to hear, but my aunt was in hysterics. Someone had fed her with horror stories of being repossessed and worse. I knew she wouldn't feel placated with any reassurances that I'd be there to take her burden. You've met her—you can see for yourself what she's like. I knew she'd only understand something emphatic like someone else saving us. She wouldn't have believed that I could get jobs and pay off the debts over time unless I was physically there to reassure her.'

Sidonie cringed when she thought of how she'd told her aunt *He's crazy about me* and looked down.

'I panicked and said the first thing I thought of.'

She looked up and Alexio's face was unreadable. Sidonie hated the suspicion that he still didn't fully believe her. But then he came and sat down on a chair near the couch and looked at her.

'Will you tell me what happened with your mother?'

Sidonie was about to blurt out that it was none of his business and then she felt those delicate flutters in her abdomen again. *Their daughter.* He had a right to the full story.

She sighed deeply. She'd never told anyone about this before. Feeling it might be easier to talk without Alexio's cool gaze on her, Sidonie stood up and went to the window, arms hugging her midriff.

'She was born in the suburbs. She and my aunt had an extremely impoverished upbringing. Their father ran out on my grandmother, leaving her to raise two daughters on her own—one with special needs My grandmother had drink problems…mental health issues…depression. Neglect was a feature of their lives. She died when my mother was about seventeen. She had to look after Tante Josephine full-time then…which she resented. She was young and bright. Beautiful. She craved opportunities beyond the grim reality of the suburbs.'

Sidonie turned round.

'My mother never told me much, but Tante Josephine's told me enough for me to know that it was pretty tough. When my mother was twenty she won a local beauty competition. Part of the prize was a trip to Dublin for the next round. She went and never came back, leaving my aunt to fend for herself on social protection in their mother's flat.

That's why my father bought her the apartment when he could. He always felt sorry for her—for how my mother had treated her…'

Shame rose up within Sidonie but she forced it down and kept looking at Alexio, determined not to allow her mother's shame to be *her* shame.

'My father was the married man my mother had the affair with—*not* the man she ended up marrying. He owned the language school where she'd signed up to do an English course with the prize money from the competition. When he found out she was pregnant he dumped her. She never forgave him for it. My stepfather met my mother around the same time. He was crazy about her and stepped in and offered to marry her.'

Sidonie's chin lifted imperceptibly.

'She was avaricious and selfish. No one knows that better than me and my aunt. And my stepfather, who stood by her despite the public humiliation she put him through. She put us all through hell when she ended up being prosecuted, and yet my stepfather never once let me feel anything less than his own child. She was put in jail for two years when I was eight years old. I had to endure taunts at school every day, because we couldn't afford to move until she was released from prison.'

Sidonie's voice shook with passion.

'I spent my whole life dreading someone finding out about her past. That's why I don't talk about it. But I am *not* her, and you had no right to assume I was like her—no matter what evidence you thought you had…'

She recalled one of the things he'd hurled at her. 'Not even the fact that I told you I liked jewellery. I'm a woman, Alexio. A lot of women like glittery shiny things. It doesn't mean we're all inveterate gold-diggers.'

Alexio stood up too, and immediately a flare of awareness made Sidonie take a step back. His eyes flashed at her movement and something tightened between them.

His mouth was a grim line. 'I'm sorry that I didn't give you the chance to tell me this, for misjudging you and for leaving you to go through what you have for the past few months. You should never have had to deal with this on your own…'

The lines of his face grew stark and his voice roughened.

'But I'm not sorry you're pregnant. I want this baby too.'

He came closer and everything in Sidonie tightened with anticipation. She tried to ignore it.

Heavily, Alexio continued, 'I should tell you why I jumped to such conclusions. My mother was the most cynical person I've ever known. She taught me not to trust at an early age, and the world and my peers have only confirmed her lesson. I'm used to lovers as cynical as I have become. You were so different from anyone I've ever met before…'

His words resounded in Sidonie's head, shocking her. She felt weakened by this mutual confessional. The hard knot of tension and pain inside her felt as if it was dissolving, treacherously.

Alexio went on. 'My parents' marriage was not happy. It was sterile, loveless. I told you why I decided to break with my father…but there's more to it than that. Once he beat my mother. I rushed in to stop him, to protect her, but she put me out of the room and went back in and closed the door, shutting me out.'

Alexio's mouth twisted.

'She didn't want or need my protection—not even then… And that's why I wanted nothing more to do with my father.'

Sidonie's heart clenched. She felt increasingly vulnerable and was aware that only inches separated them now. When had they even moved that close?

Alexio's hand closed around one upper arm, warm against her bare skin, setting off a chain reaction.

'I'm sorry, Sidonie. Truly.'

Something moved between them. Something fragile and yet something very earthy too.

But Sidonie was reeling. It was too much. She pulled her arm free and said weakly, 'I'm tired now. I should go to bed.'

Alexio just looked at her in the soft glow of the lamps. 'Yes.'

Sidonie knew she should move, but for a second she couldn't seem to. All she could see was that mouth, and all she could think about was how she wanted to feel it on hers right now. She had to get out of there before she did something stupid. Exposed herself.

Backing away, eyes huge, as if she was afraid he might pounce on her, Sidonie left the room and shut herself inside her bedroom. Her heart was beating as rapidly as if she'd just run a mile. Alexio's words swirled in her head and every cell in her body was protesting at being out of his proximity.

Trying her best to ignore the insistent throbbing of her blood and pulse, Sidonie washed herself and put on her nightshirt, got into bed. But as soon as she lay down she knew sleep was an impossibility.

She clenched her hands into fists. It was as if his words had unlocked something tight and painful inside her and replaced it with pure desire. She needed Alexio with an almost physical pain. Hunger for him made her grit her jaw. Hormones were flooding her body, stronger than anything she'd felt before.

Almost without thinking, operating on some very base level, Sidonie got out of bed and opened the door of her bedroom. She went back into the drawing room and saw Alexio standing at the window, looking like a remote fig-

ure. For a second she hesitated, but then he turned round…
and she was no more capable of going back than she was
of ceasing breathing.

Rawly, she blurted out, 'I need you to make love to me.'

Alexio thought he was dreaming. He saw Sidonie silhou-
etted in the light of a nearby lamp. Her flimsy nightshirt
clearly showed the shape of her body and the fact that she
wore no underwear. His blood boiled, blanking his brain
of everything he'd been thinking about. Lust surged, making him so hard it hurt.

Her breasts looked bigger, he could see the swell of her
belly, and something deeply primal within him exulted
fiercely. *His* seed in her belly. After their conversation he'd
been feeling ridiculously exposed, but that was incinerated
by the heat he felt right now.

Fearing she might disappear, Alexio instructed her
throatily, 'Come here.'

Sidonie moved with endearing jerkiness, and then she
was in his arms and Alexio's mouth was on hers. Her body
was pressing into him so hard it felt as if he'd be branded
with her shape for ever and he was devouring her…and
wondering dimly how he'd survived for as long as he had
without this.

Sidonie groaned deep in her throat as sheer wanton pleasure
burned up inside her at the feel of Alexio's arms around her
again, his mouth on hers, his tongue stroking hers.

She barely noticed him lifting her up into his arms, feeling weightless as she wrapped her arms around his neck
and sank deeper and deeper into the kiss. They only broke
apart so that Alexio could lay Sidonie down on his bed,
and she looked up at him as he pulled off his shirt, revealing the hard-muscled perfection of his torso. He looked
leaner, harder than she remembered, and everything feminine within her sighed voluptuously.

He took off his trousers and underwear and he was unashamedly naked and aroused. The dusky light from outside bathed him in a golden glow.

'I need to see you.' His voice was hoarse.

Sidonie's body was on fire. She couldn't remember feeling so desperate, so sensitised. Her breasts were literally throbbing, aching with need. And between her legs she felt damp and hot.

She sat up slightly and pulled her nightshirt off, but her hands were awkward.

Alexio said roughly, 'I'll do it.'

He reached down and pulled it up and then all the way off. She was naked but she couldn't drum up any embarrassment. She needed him too badly.

She could see Alexio's jaw tighten as his eyes devoured her. And then his gaze moved down to the swell of her belly. She lay back on the bed, her breathing tortured. Alexio moved between her legs, forcing them apart slightly, and then came down, resting over her on his hands. Sidonie put her hands on his arms and he bent his head again, kissing her deeply, intimately. His tongue stabbed deep, sliding along hers, making her moan with need.

When his mouth moved across her jaw and down further Sidonie's nipples tightened unbearably. Torturously slowly he came closer and closer to that distended hard tip, and when he drew it into his mouth and suckled she cried out. It hadn't been like this before. This intense.

His hand was cupping her other breast, kneading it gently, fingers pinching that peak. Sidonie's hands were in his hair, clasping him to her with a death grip. When his mouth left her breast and his head moved down Sidonie let out a gasp of disappointment which quickly turned to something else when he pressed a kiss to her belly. For a second her desire was eclipsed by something much more profound and dangerously tender.

Before she could dwell on it Alexio was moving lower, spreading her legs wide, his breath feathering across the incredibly sensitised nerves between her legs. She had to put her fist to her mouth to stop from crying out again when his mouth covered her. His tongue swirled and suckled with merciless and expert precision until she couldn't hold it back and a flood of ecstasy rushed through her in unstoppable waves.

The intensity of her orgasm left Sidonie trembling all over and she had a moment of *déjà vu*, remembering her first time with Alexio and how intense it had been. He loomed over her now, broad and awe-inspiring, and she wanted him deep inside her with a ferocious urgency that made her feel desperate.

Sidonie hooked her legs around his thighs, drawing him closer.

He emitted a guttural, 'I don't want to hurt you...the baby...'

'You won't,' she assured him breathlessly.

With a low groan, Alexio pressed closer, and then she felt the thick head of his erection sliding into her. So big.

Sidonie let out a sound of frustration, needing more, drawing him even closer, and then with one powerful thrust he sheathed himself deep within her tight, slick body. Tears of emotion sprang into Sidonie's eyes and she closed them fiercely in case Alexio might see the betraying glitter.

He was moving now—slowly, ruthlessly, in and out. The ride was slow and intense. Tension tightened inside Sidonie, making her moan and plead incoherently for Alexio to never stop.

When her climax approached Sidonie's eyes flew open. She could only see Alexio's green gaze boring into her. He held her suspended on the crest of the wave until he thrust one last time and her whole body convulsed with pleasure around his.

* * *

At some point, in the silvery glow of the moon, Sidonie woke up to feel Alexio behind her, pressing kisses to the back of her neck, making her shiver with renewed arousal. He bent over her, scooping her back against him, coming behind her, a hand reaching to find her breast and cup it, making her moan with sleepy and delicious desire.

He said softly beside her ear, 'Come up on your knees.'

Sidonie was wide awake now, and practically panting with need. Just like that—within seconds. She did as he asked and came up on her knees, her legs spread. Her upper body was on the bed, her elbows bent. Alexio stretched over her back and she could feel his steel-hard erection move against her. He took her arms and stretched them over her head. Her hands automatically gripped the pillow.

And then his thighs were behind hers, his legs moving hers even further apart. Like this, she felt unbelievably exposed and wanton. And yet never more aroused. He drew his hand down her spine, fingers tracing her bones, and then his hands spread around her hips, drawing her back and into him.

She turned her cheek to the bed. Her hands tightened to white knuckles when she felt one hand move between them to explore how ready she was. She could have wept when she felt the tremor run through his body on feeling the evidence of her desire.

Taking his hand away, he replaced it with his potent erection, and as he thrust deep and started the relentless slide of his body in and out of hers again Sidonie felt as if she was losing it completely. All that control she'd held on to for four months, the hatred… It was being washed away and leaving her vulnerable, defenceless. Raw.

Alexio's body moved with awesome power, wresting away Sidonie's ability to think rationally. When he bent close over her back and drew her hair aside, so that he could press a kiss to her exposed skin and cup her breast, she couldn't hold on any more and shattered to pieces for a third time.

When Alexio woke in the early dawn light he kept his eyes closed for a minute, relishing the hum of satisfaction in his body. Slowly, though, the satisfaction faded as memories took over.

Alexio opened his eyes and realised he was alone in his bed. If not for the crumpled sheets and that hum in his body he might have imagined that he'd had another night of dreams so vivid he woke up aching and aroused.

But sleeping with Sidonie had been no dream. It had surpassed any mere dream. She was more than he remembered—even more responsive.

Why had she left him? Suddenly irritated at the empty bed, Alexio threw back the covers and jumped out. He pulled on a pair of discarded jeans nearby, left them open, and prowled through the apartment to Sidonie's room. The door was shut. He opened it softly and went in. His heart clenched. She was in her nightshirt, lying on her side, with her legs pulled up. Long golden copper hair was spread out around her head. Lashes were long and dark against her flushed cheeks. Her breaths were deep and even.

He stood transfixed for a long moment and realised with a creeping sense of fatality that everything he'd ever known or believed in had spectacularly blown up in his face.

Yet even now he could hear his mother's cold voice in his head, mocking him: *'It's all an act, Alexio...she's fooling you even now, making you want her. Making you believe that she'd do anything but take your money when she has your baby in her belly, the best insurance a woman can get...'*

Alexio blocked out the voice with an effort. He couldn't believe he'd told Sidonie *everything* last night. The darkest, dirtiest secret of his father's violence. He'd never even told Rafaele about that. He'd never forget his mother's beautiful face, bruised and battered. But she hadn't cried out. She hadn't let him help. She'd put him from the room and closed the door and contained the incident. Always so cold, so frigid.

He could feel the remnants of the same rigidity that he'd learned from her in him, and also the desire to let it loosen. He thought of everything Sidonie had told him last night. He believed her. He *wanted* to believe her. But some deep part of him was clinging to the tentacles of the past like a drowning man clinging to a buoy.

One thing was for sure: there was no way she could not agree to the fact that Alexio was going to be an integral part of her life from now on—and his daughter's.

When Sidonie woke the following morning her whole body felt deliciously lethargic and sated. And then her eyes opened and horror coursed through her. *Alexio*. She'd begged him to make love to her last night like some kind of lust-crazed wanton.

She cringed. But then she recalled their conversation and that sensation of something giving way inside her, melting. In the cold light of day, and after what had happened last night, Sidonie couldn't keep pretending to herself that she hated Alexio. Far from it.

She'd fallen for him on Santorini—if not as early as that first night in London. *Who was she kidding?* she castigated herself. She'd probably fallen for him on that plane, before they'd even kissed. And, yes, she'd hated him for the way he'd treated her, but she'd really never stopped falling for him.

And after what he'd told her about his mother and his father... It didn't excuse him, but it made her weak heart want to empathise with how a man had become so cynical at such a young age and never had any experience to counteract that.

No wonder he'd checked himself and doubted what was going on between them if he'd never allowed a woman that close before…

Feeling dangerously dreamy all of a sudden, Sidonie got out of bed and took a shower, all at once eager to see Alexio and cursing herself for having left his bed because she'd felt so raw and exposed.

Since he'd come back into her life he'd done nothing but support her, and had taken the news of her pregnancy on board with admirable equanimity. And what had she done? Thrown everything back in his face…scared in case he got close enough to see how deep her feelings ran for him. Scared in case he'd see how flimsy that hatred was because she knew she still loved him and hated her own weakness.

He'd paid off the debts to ease her aunt's mind and to take the burden of pressure off *her*. And even though that still made Sidonie feel uncomfortable she knew that he'd undoubtedly done it out of concern for her health and the baby's.

Those debts were a drop in the ocean for him, But she was still concerned enough to make a case for paying him back. The thought of just letting him pay off debts her mother had been responsible for made Sidonie feel faintly ill.

But after last night—surely something had shifted between them? Maybe something of what they'd had before hadn't been irretrievably lost…?

Sidonie's heart beat fast at that. Maybe the lines of communication could be a little more open now. Surely he would respect her desire to pay him back?

When Sidonie went in search of Alexio and found him reading a newspaper at the breakfast table she had a smile on her face. It soon faded, though, when he looked at her with a cool expression, his face unreadable.

'Good morning.'

'Morning...' she said faintly, wondering if this clean-shaven epitome of elegance in a dark suit and shirt was the same man who had driven her to the brink of her endurance three times last night. Now she didn't feel so bad about leaving his bed. The sense of rawness and vulnerability was back with a vengeance.

The housekeeper who worked for a few hours every day, preparing meals and cleaning the apartment, bustled in with breakfast for Sidonie and she sat down silently. The doctor had recommended a diet full of nutrients to help her get back on her feet but she couldn't stomach anything now. She felt a little sick.

'Okay?' Alexio's question was cool.

Sidonie nodded and avoided his eye, picking at the food. It was as if nothing had happened.

He finished his coffee and put his paper down. 'We should talk...' he said.

Sidonie gave up pretending to try and eat and pushed her plate away slightly. She looked at him and wished she could block out the images from the previous night. The way he'd looked so intense... And she wished she could block out her feelings too, but it seemed as if now she'd admitted how she felt to herself she'd opened a dam.

'Talk about what?'

Alexio looked serious. 'About us...where we go from here.'

Something went cold inside Sidonie. She'd imagined a conversation like this, but not with Alexio sounding as if he was about to discuss profits and losses. Foolishly she'd imagined something altogether more passionate.

In her silence, he clarified, 'We can't go on in this state

of limbo… You're feeling better. I have to get back to work. We need to figure out the logistics.'

Limbo. Was that what he thought last night had been about? While Sidonie had been realising how much she loved him?

She slid out of her chair and stood up. Alexio stood too, instantly dwarfing her. She moved back.

'I don't think I'm quite getting your meaning.'

His hands curled around the back of his chair. 'What I'm talking about is where we'll live—how we will proceed. I'll have to buy a new house, of course. The apartment isn't suitable for a baby… Or maybe you want to be here? Near to your aunt?'

Sidonie's mouth had fallen open at the way he'd laid everything out so starkly. There was no emotion involved. She recovered her wits and felt anger rising at his cool arrogance.

'This baby is not *logistics*—it's a baby. Our daughter.'

Those words pricked her heart. She put her hands on her belly, the by now nearly constant fluttering comforting her.

'I don't expect *us* to *proceed* anywhere. I do expect *me* to go on with *my* life, though.'

Alexio looked every inch the powerful tycoon in that moment. 'This isn't up to you, Sidonie. You *will* allow me to provide for you and the baby.'

Sidonie cursed herself for ever having cast him in the role of benign benefactor. Emotions bubbled over. Enough for the both of them.

'Her name is Belle. Not *the baby*. And I stupidly thought that after last night something had changed…that—' She stopped and cursed herself silently. She'd said too much.

Alexio looked disgusted. 'Our daughter is *not* going to be called Belle—what kind of a name is that?'

Sidonie replied faintly, 'It's Tante Josephine's favourite name.'

She felt dazed at how naïve she'd been. *Again*. Nothing had changed.

That green gaze narrowed on her. 'You thought *what* had changed?'

Sidonie shook her head, feeling sick at how she'd almost given herself away. Disgusted with herself for allowing some confessional conversation and some hot sex to melt away her feelings of anger. She'd only ever been a transitory visitor through Alexio's bed. And now he was stuck with her.

'Nothing. I'm not doing this, Alexio—committing to some sterile arrangement just for your benefit.'

'We desire each other. Last night proved that beyond a doubt.'

Sidonie felt as exposed as if he'd just stripped her naked. A few hours ago he had.

Lifting her chin, she said tautly, 'That was hormones.'

Alexio looked comically confused for a moment. 'Hormones?'

Sidonie nodded, desperate to convince him that he had it wrong. 'It's in my pregnancy book—you can read about it. It's very common for pregnant women to feel more…' Sidonie faltered. In spite of her best efforts she blushed fiercely. 'More…amorous. It's because of all the extra blood.'

The confusion left Alexio's face and now he looked livid. A muscle throbbed in his temple. 'Hormones…? *Extra blood*? That was chemistry—pure and simple.' He was almost roaring now. 'Are you trying to tell me that any man would have done to satisfy your urges last night?'

Sidonie's face burned, but valiantly she affected as much insouciance as she could and with a small shrug reiterated, 'I'm just telling you what's in my pregnancy book.'

Alexio's face was rigid with rejection, and even she felt the sting of her conscience.

'You wanted me as much as I wanted you. There might have been extra hormones involved, but it was inevitable.'

Sidonie cursed silently. So much for hoping to convince Alexio that any man would have done. *As if.* Even now she wanted him, in spite of his being so arrogant that she wanted to hit him.

Sidonie clenched her hands into fists and glared at him for making her love him. For making her want him. For humiliating her.

'Nothing has changed, Alexio. We're exactly where we were when you arrived in Paris. The only difference now is that I owe *you* money instead of a bank.'

Alexio looked livid again. 'Stop saying that. You owe me nothing. I want to try and make this work, Sidonie.'

Sidonie felt bitter. '*This* is not a car, Alexio. And I can tell you that it's not working. Desire or no desire. That's not enough. I won't allow you to put me and our daughter up like some kind of discarded mistress and her child. I am not a sponger. I will work to pay my way for me and my child, like millions of other women around the world.'

Alexio's mouth was a tight line of displeasure. 'Millions of other women around the world haven't had the sense to fall pregnant by a billionaire.'

Sidonie gasped and went pale as his unspoken words throbbed silently between them: *So stop pretending that you don't want my support.*

Alexio immediately put out a hand. 'Sid…wait. I didn't mean it like—'

Sidonie cut him off with ice in her voice, even as her heart was breaking all over again. 'I've already told you *not* to call me that. My name is Sidonie. And you've said quite enough. You still don't trust me, do you?'

She saw the flare of guilt in his eyes and something inside her withered and died. She couldn't say another word.

She shook her head and backed away, and then turned and walked out of the room.

Alexio watched her go and then tunnelled his hands through his hair. He closed his eyes and repeated every curse he'd ever heard under the sun. Watching the way she'd gone pale just now... Something inside him had curdled and now he felt the acrid taste of panic. That hadn't gone at all the way he'd expected it to.

As if one moment of this relationship with this woman had *ever* gone the way he'd expected it to...

From the moment she'd appeared at breakfast with that shy smile Alexio had felt the dam of emotion inside him threatening to burst free. But he wasn't ready yet. It was too much.

When he came out of the dining room he saw Sidonie putting on her coat and lifting her bag. The panic escalated, making him feel constricted, rudderless. As if he were freefalling from a great height.

'Where are you going?'

Sidonie avoided his eye. 'I said I'd go over to Tante Josephine's this morning.'

She looked at him then, but there was no expression on her face or in her eyes. She was pale. The swell of her belly was visible under her top. Alexio had a sudden urge to beg Sidonie not to go, but something held him back. The memory of his mother's cold face when he'd blurted out, *Why can't you love each other?* Those tentacles were dragging him back, stronger than he could resist.

He assured himself he was overreacting. Sidonie would be back this afternoon and they would talk again. When he'd regained some sense of being in control. He was still shaking with rage at the insinuation that she would have slept with any willing red-blooded man last night because she'd just been horny.

'My car and driver are outside if you want to use them.'

Sidonie said a quiet, 'Okay.' And then she opened the door and left. Alexio had the awful sensation that even while he was so intent on retaining control he was losing it anyway.

Alexio spent the morning and early afternoon on the phone to his offices in London and Athens. But he couldn't get his poisonous words to Sidonie out of his head: *Millions of other women around the world haven't had the sense to fall pregnant by a billionaire*. Or how stricken she had looked after he'd said them. She'd looked that stricken on Santorini.

A cold fist seemed to be squeezing his heart.

His solicitor Demetrius rang and asked him, 'When are you going to stop playing nursemaid and come back to work?'

A volcanic rage erupted deep inside Alexio as he recalled how this man, *his friend,* had unwittingly fed Alexio's deeply cynical suspicions four months ago, and he slammed the phone down before he could say or do something he might regret. Like fire him. Alexio had no one to blame but himself.

He looked at the phone belligerently. The fact was that he had no desire for work. He had desire only for one thing and he was very much afraid that he had just let that one thing slip out of his grasp.

He picked up the phone again and dialled. After a few seconds a recording of Sidonie's voice sounded in his ear: *'I'm sorry I can't take your call. Leave me a message and I'll get back to you.*

Short, economical. Up-front. Alexio felt sick, and the back of his neck prickled. He didn't leave a message. He made another call and asked Tante Josephine if Sidonie had left her yet.

Tante Josephine answered him and the panic rose high enough in his throat to strangle him.

He forced himself to sound calm. 'When did she leave?'

She told him and Alexio did rapid calculations in his head. Somehow he managed to get out something vaguely coherent and then he put down the phone and stood up. And then he sat down again abruptly. Alexio didn't know what to do, and he was filled with a sense that for the first time in his largely charmed life he couldn't predict the outcome with his usual arrogance.

An image of his brother Rafaele came into his mind's eye, and he recalled how turbulent his emotions had been at seeing his brother embrace love and a family. Alexio realised now that he'd been poisonously jealous of his brother. Jealous of what he'd reached out for when everything in his life should have told him it wasn't possible.

Something was swelling inside Alexio's chest now—something bigger than the past. And with it came the fear that had held him back that morning. But for the first time Alexio didn't fight it. And then he felt another very fledgling feeling take hold: *hope*. Did he dare to think that he too could reach out and take hold of something he'd once believed in? Even if there might be nothing on the other side?

With a grim sense of resolve, and knowing that he just didn't have a choice any more, Alexio made the first of a series of calls and then instructed his driver to have the car ready.

CHAPTER TEN

SIDONIE SAT IN her seat, legs tucked up beneath her, and looked out of the small oval window of the plane. A faint heat haze shimmered off the tarmac outside. She felt bad about leaving her aunt behind, even if she *had* assured Sidonie she was fine. She was going to Dublin to enquire about getting back onto the college programme for her final year.

But then she felt the flutters in her belly and panic gripped her. How could she be thinking of going back to college when she was due to have her baby before Christmas? Tears pricked her eyes. She cursed her impetuousness. She hadn't really thought this through at all. She'd just wanted to get far away from Paris and Alexio's ongoing mistrust before he reduced her to rubble.

She couldn't believe she'd left herself wide open to his cynicism again.

She heard the sound of the air hostess saying, 'Your seat, sir.'

Sidonie's heart stopped for a moment and she looked around. An incredible sense of disappointment lanced her when she saw a small, very rotund man, sweating profusely, taking off his jacket before he sat down. She looked away, cursing herself again. What had she been hoping for? For history to repeat itself and Alexio to turn up when she wasn't even on one of his planes?

Sidonie choked back the tears and told herself that she was the biggest idiot on earth for letting her defences down so spectacularly. She bundled up her sweatshirt and put it under her head against the window, hoping to block everything out—including the take-off and landing and disturbing images of a cynical expression that softened only in passion.

'I'm sorry, sir, I'm afraid we've made a mistake with your seat. I'll have to move you.'

Sidonie woke up and blinked, surprised to see that they were in the air and she'd missed the take-off. Then she recalled why she was so tired and scowled at the memory. The air hostess was helping the man beside her out of his seat and apologising profusely while he complained vociferously.

Sidonie didn't mind. His elbow had been digging into her, and if no one else sat down she could—

'Is this seat taken?'

Sidonie stopped dead in the act of laying out her sweatshirt on the seat beside her as a pillow. She went hot and then cold. She looked up.

Alexio. In a dark suit and shirt. Looking dishevelled and a little wild.

In a daze, half wondering if she might be hallucinating, she said, 'Well, I was hoping that it would stay empty.'

Alexio grimaced. 'I'm sorry, it would appear that all the seats are taken. This is the only one left.'

Sidonie lifted up her sweatshirt and held it to her like protection. She tried to ignore the jump in her pulse at the way Alexio slipped off his jacket and sat down, infusing the small space with his scent and magnetism. The sense of *déjà vu* was heady.

Her eyes narrowed on him. She was wide awake now.

'How did you know where I was?' And then she answered herself. 'Tante Josephine.'

Alexio's mouth quirked but the smile didn't reach his eyes and for the first time Sidonie saw something in their depths she'd never seen before: nervousness. It made her pulse leap even more.

'Yes.'

Sidonie shook her head and tried to stave off the emotional pain of seeing him again—especially here. 'What do you want, Alexio?'

He shrugged minutely and looked tortured, and then he said, 'You…and our daughter.'

Sidonie fought back the tears and bit her lip before saying, 'I know you do. You feel a duty, a sense of responsibility…but it's not enough. I won't be that woman who takes from you just because you're the father of my child. And you don't trust me…'

Alexio's eyes burned fiercely now. He angled his body towards Sidonie, cocooning her from the rest of the plane. He took her hand and she could feel his trembling slightly. It stopped her from pulling back.

'I do trust you, Sid…*Sidonie*…'

Sidonie's heart clenched at the way he'd corrected himself.

His grip on her hand tightened. 'I *do*. I should never have said what I said earlier. It was stupid and I'm an ass. I didn't mean it for a second. It was a reflex. I was still clinging on to the last tiny piece of my cynical soul because I was too scared to let my past go… I was nine when my mother told me not to believe in love, that it was a fairytale. I watched her and my father annihilate each other all my life… I thought that was normal. I always chose women who were emotionally aloof…who demanded nothing. Because I had nothing to give. And then I met you, and for the first time I wanted more.'

His mouth twisted with self-recrimination.

'And yet at the first opportunity I chose to mistrust you, and then I turned my back on you…telling myself that I'd been a fool to expect anything more.'

Feeling shaky and light-headed, Sidonie said, 'That phone call was very bad luck…'

Alexio's mouth was still tight. 'But I gave you no chance to defend yourself—and why would you want to after I'd had you investigated like a common criminal?'

Sidonie wanted to touch his jaw but she held back. This moment felt very fragile. 'I can't escape the fact that my mother *was* a criminal. That's pretty damning, even if you hadn't overheard me talking to Tante Josephine. That's partly why I agreed with you when you asked if I'd set out to seduce you once I knew who you were… I felt it was hopeless…'

'The last four months have felt pretty hopeless.' Alexio's voice was bleak.

Sidonie said quietly, 'You were the first person I'd trusted in a really long time—if ever—and you hurt me…'

Contrition made Alexio's face look old all of a sudden. He went grey. 'I know. And I don't expect you to forgive me… But I wanted to tell you something.'

Sidonie looked at him and her belly hollowed out. 'What?'

His hand tightened on hers. His voice was so rough and his accent so strong that she almost couldn't make out what he was saying.

'I've fallen in love with you.'

His words dropped between them. Sidonie struggled to believe she hadn't dreamt them up.

He smiled, and it was almost sad. 'I think I fell for you on that plane…' His smile faded. 'If you give me a chance I'll spend the rest of my life making it up to you…'

Sidonie shrank back, pulling her hand free. She shook

her head, everything within her trying to dampen down the incredibly sweet swelling of joy. The fall would be too great if—

'You can't mean it…you're just saying that.'

Alexio looked fierce and affronted. 'I've never, ever said that to another woman and I never intend to.'

Sidonie felt a mix of tears and laughter vying for supremacy. But still she couldn't afford to believe. Visions of her stepfather's sad face came back to haunt her. Sad because he'd loved his wife his whole life when she hadn't loved him. Even though he'd sacrificed so much to be there for her. Alexio was saying this…but he couldn't love her as much as she loved him.

'You don't…don't mean it,' she got out, too scared to hope for even a second.

Alexio reached for her and put his hands on the bottom of her top, pulling it up to reveal her belly. Sidonie squeaked with shock, but before she could stop him Alexio was putting his big hands on her, spanning the small compact swell, and he was bending down, his mouth close to her bump, saying with a none too steady voice, 'Belle…I'm doing my best, here, to convince your mother that I love her and trust her and want to spend the rest of my life with her…and you…but it's not going so well. I don't think she believes me.'

Sidonie felt a very definite kick then—the first proper kick apart from the flutters. In shock, her eyes wide, she watched as Alexio came back up, his hands still on her belly.

There was a look of wonder on his face. 'I felt that…'

And then the look cleared, to be replaced with one of determination.

'Belle is clearly on my side. It's two against one.'

Sidonie couldn't prevent the tears from clogging her throat and flooding her eyes. She was overwhelmed by

Alexio's hands on her belly, the baby kicking for the first time...him saying he loved her.

But she ignored all that for a moment and choked out, 'I thought you said we couldn't call her Belle...'

Alexio smiled, and this time it looked slightly less nervous. 'It's growing on me—and Tante Josephine will never forgive me if we call her something else. But next time it's my choice.'

'Next time?' Sidonie choked out through even more tears.

Alexio was just a blur now, and his hands left her belly to come up and cup her face, thumbs wiping at her tears.

'Next time...if you'll have me,' he said gently, 'And the next time and the next time...'

And then his mouth was on hers and Sidonie was shaking too much to do anything but submit and allow herself the first sliver of belief that this was real and that Alexio meant what he was saying.

When he pulled back Sidonie's mouth tingled. His hands were still on her jaw, cupping her face. She looked into his eyes, searching, and all she could see there was pure... *emotion*. For the first time. No shadows. No cynicism.

She took a deep shaky breath. 'Alexio...'

'Yes...?'

'I love you too...even though you really hurt me. I fell for you when we first met and I never stopped. I'm still falling. Every time I look at you. I told myself I hated you...but I couldn't.'

Alexio's hands tightened around her and his gaze grew suspiciously bright. 'You love me?'

Sidonie wanted to take a snapshot of this moment. Alexio Christakos, multi-billionaire and playboy. Arrogance and confidence personified. Eyes shining with tears, doubting her word.

She reached up to touch his face, feeling the spiky

prickle of his stubble. He was a different man from the one who had so coolly laid out his plan that morning. He'd been hiding all this emotion. Suppressing it.

'Of course I love you. I love you so much that I'm terrified I love you more than you love me.'

Alexio just looked at her for a long moment and shook his head, smiling a little ruefully. 'Not possible, I'm afraid. You're getting the full force of years and years of repressed loving and then some more…'

He reached into his pocket for something, and pulled out a small black box. Sidonie looked down at it and back up.

Alexio looked nervous again. 'Sid… *Sidonie*…'

'No…' she said urgently, and then, more shyly, 'I like it when you call me that… I just… I was angry…'

She could see the pain in his eyes at that and she touched his jaw. Alexio dragged his gaze away and opened the box. Sidonie looked down and gasped when she saw a stunning heart-shaped diamond ring glittering up at her. Alexio took the ring out of the box. He took her left hand in his and looked at her so deeply that he took her breath away and made fresh tears well.

Looking endearingly unlike himself, palpably nervous, he asked, 'Will you marry me, Sidonie Fitzgerald?'

The tears overflowed and fell. Sidonie couldn't speak. She was too overcome.

Suddenly Alexio disappeared again, down towards her bump, and she heard him say, 'Belle, I've just asked—'

Alexio yelped when Sidonie grabbed his hair and pulled him back up.

'Yes!' She looked at him. 'Yes…' she said again, framing his face with her hands. 'I'll marry you, Alexio.'

Alexio kissed the palm of her hand and then took it in his again, to slide the ring onto her finger. 'I had a jeweller meet me at the plane and I picked that one out because it reminded me of your pure heart…but I can change it…'

Sidonie shook her head, looking at the ring glinting at her. 'No..' She felt more tears coming after what he'd just said. 'I love it…and it's really glittery.'

Alexio pulled her in close. 'I'll give you glittery things for the rest of our lives…'

Sidonie stiffened and pulled back, making Alexio frown.

'No… I don't want anything from you, Alexio… I mean it. I know you say you trust me, but I don't want you to ever doubt that I want nothing from you except you. I won't marry you until I can sign something that says I'm not after you for your money.'

Alexio sighed. 'Sid, don't be ridiculous.'

Sidonie pulled away and dragged her top down over her bump. She shook her head again and crossed her arms. 'No marriage unless you agree.'

Sidonie saw Alexio's eyes slide down to her bump and she put a hand over it.

'And no more cutesy manipulation of our daughter before she's even born.'

Alexio rolled his eyes heavenward and then threw up his hands. 'Okay—fine.'

His eyes glinted with determination then and he reached for her, pulling her into him so tightly that she didn't know where she ended and he began. Sidonie slid her arms around his waist and snuggled against him. They rested like that for a long moment, the calm after the storm.

'Sid?'

'Hmm?'

'Are you going to sleep?'

Sidonie nodded her head against Alexio's chest and said sleepily, happily, 'It's those hormones again. I have a feeling you're going to be keeping me up late, so I should really nap now. And also pregnant women shouldn't be subjected to too much excitement—it takes it out of us.'

She felt Alexio tense slightly and heard his affronted,

'What happened last night was more than hormones and you know it. Luckily we have the rest of our lives for me to prove it to you…'

The rest of our lives…

Sidonie smiled and moved closer to Alexio, deeper into his embrace, and he moved slightly so that he could put a possessive hand over her belly, setting off a chain reaction of desire.

'Okay,' she admitted sheepishly, lifting her head to look at him. 'Maybe it wasn't just pregnancy hormones…'

Alexio cupped her jaw with his hand and looked down at her. 'Excuse my French in front of Belle,' he said with a wicked smile, 'but damn right it wasn't.'

Two days later, Dublin

'Now I just want to make absolutely sure I haven't missed any loopholes or sneaky amendments. This was all drawn up very quickly because my fiancé has arranged our marriage for two weeks' time in Paris.'

Sidonie ignored the snort of insult from the man pacing the solicitor's office. She smiled sweetly at Mr Keane, who looked as if he was having trouble holding back nervous hysterics. No doubt he hadn't expected to see one of the world's foremost self-made billionaires in his office, never mind in this position.

Sidonie went on. 'Is it absolutely clear that if we divorce—'

'There will never be a divorce,' came the fierce pronouncement.

Sidonie rolled her eyes at the solicitor and then looked at her fiancé.

'Well, of course *now* we don't think there'll be a divorce, but you never know what will happen in life and I want to make sure that if and when such a time comes I walk away with not a cent of your fortune.'

Sidonie felt absolutely sure that there would be no divorce either, but it wasn't a bad thing to keep an alpha male like Alexio on his toes.

Alexio was bristling. He stalked over and put his hands down on the desk to glare at Sidonie. The intensity of that glare was diminished somewhat by the way he looked at her mouth so hungrily.

'There will not be a divorce while there is breath in my body.'

Sidonie stretched up and pressed a kiss to Alexio's cheek, causing his expression to turn positively nuclear. 'Well, we have to get married first, of course. Don't get all excited.'

She turned and smiled again at the very flushed-looking solicitor. 'So, in the event of a divorce any children will be provided for, and custody arrangements have been outlined, but I will get nothing—is that right?'

The solicitor ran a pudgy finger underneath his collar, his gaze flicking uneasily to the man who all but towered over his pregnant fiancée. Having had a lot of experience with pregnant women, thanks to his own healthy brood of seven children, he figured the lesser of two evils right now was Alexio Christakos, even if he *was* paying his bill and practically had steam coming out of his ears.

'Yes, that's exactly it, Miss Fitzgerald.'

'And ninety per cent of the money that Mr Christakos is insisting on giving me as an allowance has been designated to the various charities I mentioned?'

The solicitor quickly scanned the pages again and said, 'Yes, I believe so.'

'Great!'

Sidonie reached over and took the pen and signed her name with a flourish. Then she smiled sweetly at Alexio and handed the pen to him. He signed on the line with much unintelligible muttering under his breath.

Two weeks later a radiant and glowing Sidonie walked down the aisle of the biggest *mairie* in Paris on the arm of her matron of honour—her aunt, who grinned from ear to ear and was resplendent in a lavender suit. It had been bought by Alexio, who had grumbled that at least he could lavish gifts on *someone*.

Alexio hadn't had to turn and see Sidonie arrive. He'd already been waiting impatiently for her to appear.

He was still unprepared, though, when she did. His breath caught and he couldn't stop the tears clogging his throat and making his eyes shine. He'd been holding his emotions back all his life and now they overflowed. And he loved it. He'd even been oblivious to his brother Rafaele's smug *welcome to the club* look.

Sidonie's hair was half up, half down, held in place with a plain diamond art deco clip. She wore no other jewellery apart from her engagement ring. Her dress was strapless and had an empire line under her bust to accommodate her growing bump. The off-white material fell in loose, unstructured folds to the floor. Her skin glowed, and as she came closer, her eyes fixed on his, his heart almost stopped at the sheer strength of his love all over again.

He held out his hand to her and she put hers in his and smiled at him. At that moment Alexio felt all the pieces of his life slide into place, and he drew the love of his life forward by his side and hoped that they could get to the kiss as fast as possible.

Outside the office of the *mairie* afterwards, Cesar da Silva thrust his hands into his pockets. It had been a mistake to come. He didn't know what had got into him, but that morning he'd seen the invitation to Alexio's wedding on his desk and something had compelled him to make the journey to Paris from Spain.

He'd arrived late and stood at the back of the civil office. Alexio and his wife had had their backs to him as the ceremony was conducted, but he'd seen his other half-brother, Rafaele, near the front, holding a small boy high in his arms, with a dark-haired woman beside him, her arm around his waist. His wife.

He'd been invited to their wedding too, just months before, but the rage within him had still been too fierce for him even to contemplate it. The rage he'd felt at finally coming face to face with his half-brothers at his mother's funeral. The rage he'd felt at the evidence that she'd loved them above him. That she hadn't abandoned *them*.

But he knew it wasn't their fault. Whatever the stain had been on Cesar's personality that had led their mother to leave him behind had nothing to do with them. Maybe, he surmised cynically, they were just more lovable.

God knew, he'd felt dark for so long he was constantly surprised that people didn't run in terror when they looked into his eyes and saw nothing light. But they didn't run. And especially not women. It seemed the darker he felt, the stronger the draw to his lovers. More than one had been under the erroneous impression that they could *heal* Cesar of the darkness in his soul.

He wasn't surprised at women's eagerness to put up with his less than sunny nature; after all he was one of the richest men in the world. His mother had taught him that lesson very early on. After cutting Cesar from her life like a useless appendage she'd gone on to feather her nest in fine style—first with an Italian count and then, after he'd lost everything, a Greek tycoon.

He could see Rafaele putting his son down now—an adorable-looking little boy. *His nephew.* Cesar felt it like a punch to his gut. He'd been about the same age when his mother had left him with his grandparents and everything had gone dark and cold. To see that small boy now, swinging between his parents' hands, was almost too much to bear.

And then his youngest half-brother Alexio emerged from the *mairie*'s office with his new wife. His *pregnant* wife. More new life unfolding.

The pain in Cesar's chest increased. They were beaming. Eyes only on each other. Besotted. Cesar could feel his blackness spreading out…infecting the people around him like a virus. He caught one or two double-takes. People were wary around him. Women were fascinated, lustful. Covetous.

It gave him no measure of satisfaction to be as blessed as his brothers in his physical appearance. It compounded his cynicism. His looks merely sweetened the prospect for avaricious lovers, and they had proved to him from an early age that women were shallow. If he had nothing they'd still want him, but they wouldn't have to put on the elaborate pretence of not being interested in his fortune. Sometimes he almost felt sorry for them, watching them contort themselves into what they thought he wanted them to be.

Alexio was lifting his new wife into his arms now. Hearing her squeal of happiness, and seeing her throw her bouquet high in the air behind her so the women could catch it, made something break apart inside Cesar. He had to get away. He shouldn't have come. He would taint this happiness with his presence.

But just as he turned someone caught his arm, and he looked back to see Rafaele, with his son in his arms. The small boy was looking at Cesar curiously and he could see that he'd inherited his grandmother's eyes. *His* eyes. He felt weak.

As if Rafaele could see and understand the wild need to escape in Cesar's chest, he said, 'Whatever you might think our lives were like with our mother…they *weren't*. I'll tell Alexio you came. Maybe we'll see you again…?'

Cesar was slightly stunned at Rafaele's words. And at the way he'd seen his need to get out of there. That he wasn't pushing for more.

His chest feeling tight, Cesar nodded and bit out, 'Give him my best wishes.'

And then he turned and walked away quickly from that happy scene, before his wondering about what Rafaele had meant about their mother could tear him open completely and expose the dried husk of his soul to the light.

* * * * *

Mills & Boon® Hardback

April 2014

ROMANCE

A D'Angelo Like No Other	Carole Mortimer
Seduced by the Sultan	Sharon Kendrick
When Christakos Meets His Match	Abby Green
The Purest of Diamonds?	Susan Stephens
Secrets of a Bollywood Marriage	Susanna Carr
What the Greek's Money Can't Buy	Maya Blake
The Last Prince of Dahaar	Tara Pammi
The Sicilian's Unexpected Duty	Michelle Smart
One Night with Her Ex	Lucy King
The Secret Ingredient	Nina Harrington
Her Soldier Protector	Soraya Lane
Stolen Kiss From a Prince	Teresa Carpenter
Behind the Film Star's Smile	Kate Hardy
The Return of Mrs Jones	Jessica Gilmore
Her Client from Hell	Louisa George
Flirting with the Forbidden	Joss Wood
The Last Temptation of Dr Dalton	Robin Gianna
Resisting Her Rebel Hero	Lucy Ryder

MEDICAL

200 Harley Street: Surgeon in a Tux	Carol Marinelli
200 Harley Street: Girl from the Red Carpet	Scarlet Wilson
Flirting with the Socialite Doc	Melanie Milburne
His Diamond Like No Other	Lucy Clark

0314GEN STD HB

Mills & Boon® Large Print

April 2014

ROMANCE

Defiant in the Desert	Sharon Kendrick
Not Just the Boss's Plaything	Caitlin Crews
Rumours on the Red Carpet	Carole Mortimer
The Change in Di Navarra's Plan	Lynn Raye Harris
The Prince She Never Knew	Kate Hewitt
His Ultimate Prize	Maya Blake
More than a Convenient Marriage?	Dani Collins
Second Chance with Her Soldier	Barbara Hannay
Snowed in with the Billionaire	Caroline Anderson
Christmas at the Castle	Marion Lennox
Beware of the Boss	Leah Ashton

HISTORICAL

Not Just a Wallflower	Carole Mortimer
Courted by the Captain	Anne Herries
Running from Scandal	Amanda McCabe
The Knight's Fugitive Lady	Meriel Fuller
Falling for the Highland Rogue	Ann Lethbridge

MEDICAL

Gold Coast Angels: A Doctor's Redemption	Marion Lennox
Gold Coast Angels: Two Tiny Heartbeats	Fiona McArthur
Christmas Magic in Heatherdale	Abigail Gordon
The Motherhood Mix-Up	Jennifer Taylor
The Secret Between Them	Lucy Clark
Craving Her Rough Diamond Doc	Amalie Berlin

Mills & Boon® Hardback
May 2014

ROMANCE

The Only Woman to Defy Him	Carol Marinelli
Secrets of a Ruthless Tycoon	Cathy Williams
Gambling with the Crown	Lynn Raye Harris
The Forbidden Touch of Sanguardo	Julia James
One Night to Risk it All	Maisey Yates
A Clash with Cannavaro	Elizabeth Power
The Truth About De Campo	Jennifer Hayward
Sheikh's Scandal	Lucy Monroe
Beach Bar Baby	Heidi Rice
Sex, Lies & Her Impossible Boss	Jennifer Rae
Lessons in Rule-Breaking	Christy McKellen
Twelve Hours of Temptation	Shoma Narayanan
Expecting the Prince's Baby	Rebecca Winters
The Millionaire's Homecoming	Cara Colter
The Heir of the Castle	Scarlet Wilson
Swept Away by the Tycoon	Barbara Wallace
Return of Dr Maguire	Judy Campbell
Heatherdale's Shy Nurse	Abigail Gordon

MEDICAL

200 Harley Street: The Proud Italian	Alison Roberts
200 Harley Street: American Surgeon in London	Lynne Marshall
A Mother's Secret	Scarlet Wilson
Saving His Little Miracle	Jennifer Taylor

Mills & Boon® Large Print
May 2014

ROMANCE

The Dimitrakos Proposition	Lynne Graham
His Temporary Mistress	Cathy Williams
A Man Without Mercy	Miranda Lee
The Flaw in His Diamond	Susan Stephens
Forged in the Desert Heat	Maisey Yates
The Tycoon's Delicious Distraction	Maggie Cox
A Deal with Benefits	Susanna Carr
Mr (Not Quite) Perfect	Jessica Hart
English Girl in New York	Scarlet Wilson
The Greek's Tiny Miracle	Rebecca Winters
The Final Falcon Says I Do	Lucy Gordon

HISTORICAL

From Ruin to Riches	Louise Allen
Protected by the Major	Anne Herries
Secrets of a Gentleman Escort	Bronwyn Scott
Unveiling Lady Clare	Carol Townend
A Marriage of Notoriety	Diane Gaston

MEDICAL

Gold Coast Angels: Bundle of Trouble	Fiona Lowe
Gold Coast Angels: How to Resist Temptation	Amy Andrews
Her Firefighter Under the Mistletoe	Scarlet Wilson
Snowbound with Dr Delectable	Susan Carlisle
Her Real Family Christmas	Kate Hardy
Christmas Eve Delivery	Connie Cox

Discover more romance at

www.millsandboon.co.uk

- ❤ WIN great prizes in our exclusive competitions
- ❤ BUY new titles before they hit the shops
- ❤ BROWSE new books and REVIEW your favourites
- ❤ SAVE on new books with the Mills & Boon® Bookclub™
- ❤ DISCOVER new authors

PLUS, to chat about your favourite reads, get the latest news and find special offers:

- Find us on facebook.com/millsandboon
- Follow us on twitter.com/millsandboonuk
- ❤ Sign up to our newsletter at millsandboon.co.uk